A MAN NAMED DOLL

ALSO BY JONATHAN AMES

FICTION

I Pass Like Night

The Extra Man

Wake Up, Sir!

You Were Never Really Here

NONFICTION

What's Not to Love?

My Less Than Secret Life

I Love You More Than You Know

The Double Life Is Twice as Good

COMICS

The Alcoholic

AS EDITOR

Sexual Metamorphosis

A MAN NAMED

Doll

JONATHAN AMES

MULHOLLAND BOOKS

LITTLE, BROWN AND COMPANY

NEW YORK BOSTON LONDON

Mulholland Books / Little, Brown and Company
Hachette Book Group
1290 Avenue of the Americas, New York, NY 10104
mulhollandbooks.com

First Edition: April 2021

Mulholland Books is an imprint of Little, Brown and Company, a division of Hachette Book Group, Inc. The Mulholland Books name and logo are trademarks of Hachette Book Group, Inc.

The publisher is not responsible for websites (or their content) that are not owned by the publisher.

The Hachette Speakers Bureau provides a wide range of authors for speaking events. To find out more, go to hachettespeakersbureau.com or call (866) 376-6591.

ISBN 978-0-316-70365-9
LCCN 2020946118

Printing 1, 2021

LSC-C

Printed in the United States of America

For Ray Pitt
(1930–2020)

PART I

1.

SHELTON HAD ALWAYS been a hard man to kill.

But this time he looked nervous.

He came to my shabby little office on a Tuesday in early March, 2019. It had been a few weeks since I'd seen him last and he didn't look good. But that wasn't unusual. He never looked good. He was covered in liver spots like a paisley tie and was built like a bowling pin—round in the middle and meager up top. His head was small.

He was in the customer's chair and I was behind my desk.

He was seventy-three, bald, and short, and getting shorter all the time.

I was fifty, Irish, and nuts, and getting nuttier all the time.

Outside there was a downpour. LA was crying and had been for weeks. The window behind my desk was being pelted; the noise was like a symphony gone mad.

It was rainy season. An old-fashioned one. An anomaly. Hadn't rained this long in years, and LA had turned Irish green: the brown, scorched hills were soft with new grass, like chest hair on a burn victim. You could almost think that everything was going to be all right with the world. Almost.

"I'm in a bad way, Hank," Shelton said. "That's why I came to see you in person. Even in this weather."

His tan raincoat was wet and splotched and looked like the greasy wax paper they use for deli meat. He fished his Pall Malls out of his right pocket and set one on fire. He knew I didn't mind, and it didn't matter anyway. Even when he wasn't smoking, he smelled like he was. His open mouth was like an idling car.

"Why you in a bad way, Lou? What's going on?" I pushed my ashtray, littered with the ends of joints, closer to his side of the desk.

"You know I lost the kidney, right?" he said.

"Yeah. Of course," I said. "I visited you. Remember?" I took a joint out of my desk drawer, struck a match, and lit up. But I knew I wouldn't get high. I've smoked too much over the years and I'm saturated with THC. So at this point, it's just a placebo. A placebo that takes the edge off. Makes the night-mare something you don't have to wake up from. You know it's all a dream. Even if it's a bad dream.

"I know. I know," Lou said. "I'm just saying. You know I lost one, and now, well, the good kidney, which wasn't that good, is going. And I'm looking at dialysis. And dialysis is a living death."

He sucked on his cigarette. Lou Shelton had been smoking two packs a day since he was fifteen. He'd had open-heart surgery three times and had more stents than fingers. He'd survived mouth cancer and throat cancer and tongue cancer, and his voice was a toss-up between a rasp, a wheeze, and a death rattle.

I'd seen him once with his shirt off, and he had a fat scar, like an ugly red snake, down the middle of his chest. It was a zipper that kept getting opened, and from being in hospitals so much, he had a more or less permanent case of MRSA, which made him prone to boils on his ass that had to be lanced.

And he sucked on the Pall Mall.

Like I said, he was a hard man to kill.

"They say it's definite? You got to do the dialysis? What is it, once a week?"

"Once a week? Are you crazy? You go every other day, sometimes every day. For hours on end. And you need help. A woman. A child. I don't have any of that."

Shelton's wife, also a heavy smoker, had died of pneumonia five years before. She had gone fast. Her lungs were shot.

They'd had one kid, a daughter, but she wouldn't see Shelton. After he lost the first kidney and wouldn't quit smoking, she cut him out of her life. Said she couldn't stand by anymore and watch him kill himself. Like mom.

Still, he sent her a nice check every month. He would never stop loving her, but I guess he loved his cigarettes more. He had a grandchild he'd never seen. And his daughter cashed the checks. Never said thank you. Why should she?

"Maybe dialysis isn't that bad," I said.

"No! It's death. I'm never gonna do it."

Part of me wanted to say, "Just give up already, Lou. You're done. You're dead. And you did it to yourself."

But who was I to deprive him—in my mind—of one more cup of coffee, one more good feeling, one more bit of happiness?

So I pulled on my joint and said, "You could at least try it. Maybe it's easier than you think. And what choice do you have?"

"No way. Remember MacKenzie from Homicide? He's on it.

Too much booze. Pickled himself. I went to see him. He's bent over like a shrimp cocktail. Can't lift his head. And nobody was tougher."

"I should give him a call," I said. But I probably wouldn't. I always put those calls off, and then the person dies. Someday somebody won't call me.

"He asked me to shoot him in the head," Lou said. "He knows I still carry. He said, 'Come on, Lou, you remember how I was. End this for me. Or just give me the piece and I'll do it myself.' I got out of there fast, and so now I'm telling everybody: I need a new kidney. I'm looking for volunteers. I'll go off these—"

He stubbed out his cigarette and lit another. His troubled eyes were a watery, cataract blue—his nicest feature—and the smoke from the new cigarette plumed out of his nose, two wispy trails, not long for this world.

"What do the doctors at the VA say?" I asked. "Can you get a transplant?"

Shelton had been in Vietnam. Got a Purple Heart. But never talked about it. Like most people, he was a mix of things. Heroic and selfish. Insightful and blind. Sane and insane.

"I asked, but they won't put me on the list," he said. "I'm not a good candidate. It'd be a waste of a kidney...but not to me."

"I'm sorry, Lou. This is rough. Real rough."

"Anyway, even if I got on the list, by the time they called my number, I'd be dead. So I gotta buy one," he said, and then added real fast, "I'll give you fifty thousand, Hank. Maybe even seventy-five, maybe more—I'm working on an angle—and I'll pay all your medical expenses. We just have to see if you're the right blood type."

Then he looked down, ashamed. I hadn't caught his meaning when he said he was looking for volunteers. "Lou, jeez. Come on," I pleaded.

"I'm serious," he said, and he lifted his head and looked at me dead-on, not scared or ashamed anymore. He'd made his ask. "I know you could use the money. I'm O positive. What are you?"

"I don't know," I said. "But who's gonna do the surgery? You can't buy an organ and then find some doctor to put it in you."

"No—I'd take you to the VA. They'll check your blood and you say you're doing it because you love me or because of God—there's a whole process—but as long as nobody knows about the money, it's totally legit. And they'd believe you, because we go way back. And because...you know."

Now it was my turn to look down.

Lou Shelton had saved my life back in '94. I was a rookie cop and he was a desk sergeant. But this one time, during a mini riot down in Inglewood, he was on the street with us. We needed extra bodies, and we were going around the alley side of a strip mall to get at some looters from behind, but they chose that moment to slip out the back, and there was a gunfight. Lou pushed me out of the way and took a bullet. Lost his spleen. The one thing not cut out of him because of the cigarettes.

But because of me.

Now he wanted one of my kidneys. Almost like a trade. I sucked on the joint. Could I do it? *Should* I do it? I didn't know what to say. So he bailed me out. "Just think about it," he said. "I know it's asking a lot."

"Okay, Lou, I will."

"And it's not all on you. Don't worry. I'm asking everybody, and I'm looking into the black market. I met this kid. A computer whiz. A Pakistani at the motel"—Lou was the night man at the Mirage Suites, a transient motel on Ventura Boulevard in North Hollywood—"knows all about what they call the dark web. You heard of it?"

"Yeah, I've heard of it. But black market? Are you crazy?"

"What the fuck you want from me?" he said, angry all of a sudden. "I'm on death row! I gotta try everything. And if *you* can't do it, you work that Asian spa. There's gotta be one of them who'd sell me a kidney. You could ask around."

"I can't do that, Lou. You're not thinking straight."

"I'd be helping them! You can start a life with fifty grand. They could stop whoring. I'd be doing more for them than you do."

I looked at Lou and put out my joint. A quiet came over us. The meanness and fire went slowly out of his eyes.

Then he said, "I'm sorry. That was a low blow. I'm not myself. But I'm desperate. I got maybe three months before this thing goes. I can feel it dying." He nodded toward his abdomen, to the kidney inside him, a water bag gone bad.

"So just think about it," he said, and stood up. "I had to ask."

"All right, Lou," I said.

He nodded and made for the door. On the other side of it was a metal plate that said: H. DOLL, INVESTIGATIONS & SECURITY. Most people call me Hank, but my real name is Happy. Happy Doll. My parents saddled me with that name. They didn't think it was a joke. They'd been hoping for the best. Can't say it worked out. Can't say it didn't.

At the door, Lou turned and looked at me. "I'm sorry about

what I said. I know you take care of those girls the best you can."

Then he straightened himself—there was still plenty of Marine and good cop left in Lou Shelton, and I caught a glimpse of it, his true self. He'd always been small and brave like a bullet, and he nodded at me and left.

I swiveled in my chair and stared out the window; it was streaked with tears. Rainy season.

2.

SHELTON LEFT AROUND five p.m. I finished my joint, locked my office, and headed out to the Dresden. The bar, not the city, and I ran up the street in the rain. The Dresden was only half a block away, and I wanted a drink. I wanted to mix some tequila with the marijuana and think about what Lou had asked of me.

The bar, which had just opened for the night, was empty, the way I like it, and the place hasn't changed much since circa 1978: long oak bar, lots of shadow, no windows, red leather booths, and a battered piano, like an old horse that still wants to please, in the middle of the floor.

I took a seat at the end of the bar, and Monica Santos, my beautiful friend, drifted over, smiling. Monica's got a long scar down the left side of her face, parts her silky brown hair down the middle, and is one of those people that has an actual twinkle in her green eyes. And I don't know what that twinkle is, exactly, but there's something in Monica's eyes that is alive. She said: "What are you drinking, Happy?"

Monica knew my real name and liked it, and I didn't protest. She had license to call me whatever she wanted.

"A child's portion of Don Julio," I said.

I always order alcohol that way—stole it from an old mentor, a cop long dead. But he used it for food because he had diverticulitis. I use it for alcohol because I'm Irish. But that's not entirely true. I'm also half Jewish. On my mother's side. I'm half Jew, half Mick, all ish. My father was a redhead and she was dark. I got his blue eyes and her black hair.

Monica gave me another smile, went off to get my drink, and as she reached for the bottle, I studied her profile. The one with the scar. Then I looked at the rest of her—she's tiny but strong. She was wearing some kind of yellow halter frock, and her bare arms looked pretty. She had recently turned thirty-eight and had been bartending a long time.

She brought me my drink and rested her hand on mine.

A few years ago, when I was heartbroken, she had taken me into her bed. In the morning, I cried about the other woman and she never slept with me again. I had squandered her love. But not her friendship. She liked my dog and looked after him on occasion. And sometimes we met for coffee. But mostly we saw each other at the bar.

She squeezed my hand and said: "You doing okay?"

"Yeah. A friend wants a kidney, but I'm good."

"What?"

"Only joking," I said.

Just then a couple of regulars, old-timers, wet from the rain, sauntered in, and Monica went to them. They all love Monica, and she loves them back. She likes broken birds, and old men are her babies, her specialty. I hoped, sitting there, that I wasn't in that category, but I may have been fooling myself.

So I took a sip of Mr. Don Julio and got off that depressing topic and moved on to another one: the pros and cons of the kidney question. I started with the cons: giving Lou a kidney, if I was the right blood type, was the definition of throwing good money after bad. How long would it last him? Two years? Less? His body was shot.

Another con was that I was a little squeamish. The idea of someone reaching into my body and taking something out made me feel funny.

I took another sip. And thought some more.

The cons ended there. At squeamish.

The pros?

Lou had saved my life. I wasn't wearing my vest that day. That .45 would have ripped right through me. Lou was wearing his vest and the bullet caught the edge of it, which blunted some of the impact, so the bullet only nicked him but still took out his spleen. And he lived. I wouldn't have made it without a vest—.45s punch holes in you that you don't come back from.

Then I took another sip.

The tequila filled in the marijuana. Liquid in smoke. And I felt good. Generous. Magnanimous. Loving of my fellow man. Loving of Lou.

And I made my decision.

I'd get my blood tested and if I was O, he could have one of my kidneys, the right or left, whichever he wanted. And free of charge. No $50K.

And where was he going to get that kind of money anyway? He didn't have any savings and his LAPD pension check went to his daughter every month. He must have been dreaming that he could come up with fifty thousand dollars.

I took out my phone to call him, but the battery was dead. I was always letting it run down. Because I hated the thing. Hated the phone. Hated being its slave and not its master.

I left Monica a twenty—I always overtip her; how can I not?—and started to head out. I was due at work at six, but I needed to stop at the house and walk the dog, and at the house, I could charge the phone. My car, a '95 Caprice Classic, was too old for that kind of thing. Charging phones. It was from a simpler time.

As I got to the back door, Monica ran to the end of the bar and called out: "Have a good night, Happy. See you soon."

"Yeah, see you soon," I said. "Probably tomorrow." And she laughed. I was in there most every day—because of her—usually around the opening bell, at five. Then she said, for no reason, kind of wistful, something she had never said before: "You know, I love you, Hap."

I just looked at her, stunned, couldn't say it back, though I wanted to, and so all I said, before stepping outside, was: "See you tomorrow."

But I didn't know then I wouldn't be back in the Dresden for a long time. I didn't know any of the bad things that were going to happen to me, and, worst of all, to Monica.

3.

I KEPT MY CAR in the lot behind the bar, and during the time it had taken me to drink my small dose of tequila, it had stopped raining and the sun, just before setting, had come out, and the light was magnificent. The world had turned purple.

I opened the windows as I drove and the air was fresh and sharp, and for a moment Los Angeles really was what the Spanish first called it: the Town of the Queen of Angels.

I headed north on Vermont and up ahead, on the mountain, the Griffith Observatory kept watch over the city, its wet dome like the head of an eagle.

I made a left onto Franklin, endured the traffic for a few lights, then made a right onto Canyon Drive in the direction of Bronson Canyon and the caves. I cut through the hills the back way and descended down to Beachwood Canyon and home. I live off of Beachwood Drive on a little dead-end street called Glen Alder. It's at the base of the hill with the big wooden sign, the one that says HOLLYWOOD.

I parked in my detached garage, a white stucco box with terra-cotta shingles, opened the gate to the fence, and started my way up the forty-five stairs to my house, a white Spanish two-story bungalow built in 1923.

It has just four small rooms and a bathroom, but it was part of the original Hollywoodland development, and it rests high above the street, lodged into the side of a small hill. My front yard, feral and overgrown, is like a bit of sloping forest.

"Hello, everyone," I said as I climbed, and I was speaking to all the trees and plants, and then in the dying light, I bent over some salvia and addressed them directly. "You're so beautiful," I said, and the thin purple tentacles swayed like underwater lilies.

I climbed some more stairs and touched one of my avocado trees—its trunk was strong and proud. Then, as I approached my house, which is shrouded by another avocado tree and a big elm, I said, "Hello, Frimma, darling," which is what I call her. My house, like a ship, is female, and then I was through the door, and my dog, George, went nuts, jumping on me.

"Hello, George," I said in English, and he said, "Hello, my great love," in dog, which is spoken with the eyes. Then I plugged in my phone in the kitchen so I could call Lou after it charged.

In the meantime, George needed a walk and I grabbed his leash, and he started jumping even higher than he had in greeting. He's half Chihuahua, half terrier of some kind, and quite springy. I've had him two years—he's a rescue; someone left him chained to a fence—and he's three or four years old, according to the vet. Unfortunately, I know nothing of his life before me, which I have to accept.

"George, sit!" I said. "Sit. Come on, sit!"

Finally, he calmed down enough for me to loop the leash around his neck and we went out the door. He was pulling hard down the stairs, but I didn't care. He'd been cooped up all day and I wanted him to feel free.

Then we hit the street and I admired, as I often do, his small, muscular torso and how sleek and handsome he is. His legs are thin and elegant, as are his long-fingered paws, and his coloring—a tan head and body and a white neck—makes him look like he's wearing a khaki suit and a white shirt, which is a good look for a gentleman like George in the semiarid clime of Los Angeles.

Trim and fit, he weighs about 22 pounds and has large mascara-rimmed eyes that break your heart and make you fall in love simultaneously.

Unlike most dog owners, I don't project onto him that he's my child, my son. Rather, it's a more disturbed relationship than that. I think of him as my dear friend whom I happen to live with. In that way, we're like two old-fashioned closeted bachelors who cohabitate and don't think the rest of the world knows we're lovers.

He does have his own bed, which I banish him to every now and then, but that's very rare, and so we sleep together most every night of the year.

He starts off with his head resting on the pillow next to me, giving me moony eyes as I read—I always read before going to bed—and then when I'm tired, I put my book down and bury my face in his neck and inhale his earthy dog smell, which I love, and then I kiss his neck like he's my wife before I turn off the light, and then he tries to put his tongue in my mouth, which I don't allow, but I let him lick the corner of my eye to get some salty crust or something else tasty—it's a whole ritual we have—and then when the lights go out, he burrows under the sheets and puts his warm body next to mine, and I'm ready to sing like Fred Astaire: "Heaven. I'm in heaven…"

So we walked down to Beachwood and then over to Glen Holly and back; he had one nicely formed bowel movement and at least two dozen marking urinations. Back inside, I filled his bowl with his food and made a quick plate for myself—a pickle, some crackers, some sauerkraut, and a can of mackerel whipped up with some Vegenaise.

Some intrepid ants were crawling around on the counter as I prepared this feast, but I didn't have the heart to kill them. They were going about their business with such great purpose and industriousness that it seemed unfair to just come along and crush them. They had things to do! And I hate to kill anything.

So I took my plate into the small living room, where I have an old wooden table, and ate quickly. The pickle and the sauerkraut I thought of as my vegetables and my fiber, and the mackerel was my protein.

My eating habits are odd but healthy.

I was out of the house and headed down the stairs by 6:10, and George went out to his little wire enclosure, off the kitchen, to say goodbye. There's a doggie door in the kitchen door, and the eight-foot enclosure beyond it—like a chicken coop—lets George get some fresh air when he wants to while keeping him protected from coyotes. He can also use it as a pissoir when necessary.

"Goodbye, George," I said, and his eyes were sad, but I steeled myself and didn't look back.

As I drove to work, I left Lou a message. Being even more old school than I am, he didn't have a cell phone but a landline with an answering machine; he lived in a small unit of the

Mirage, which came with a kitchenette and its own phone. He'd been living there for about ten years and the room was a perk of his job as the night man at the motel.

The answering machine made a beep—there was no outgoing message—and I said: "Lou, it's Hank. Thought about what we talked about. I'd like to do it. Let's go to the VA and find out if we match."

Then I paused. I almost said "I love you," but I didn't. I just said, "So call me," and hung up. I have no problem telling George or the plants or the trees in my yard or my house that I love them, but with people it doesn't come so easy.

4.

MY NIGHT JOB was at the Thai Miracle Spa, on the second floor of a two-story strip mall at the corner of Argyle and Franklin, not far from my house.

I got there at 6:20, and Mrs. Pak, the owner, was working the desk. She lowered her reading glasses to give me a look but didn't say anything. She was in her midsixties, but her hair was still lustrous and black, like oil. She was always very serious, but when she smiled, which was rare, she was radiant. That night, she was wearing a man's white shirt, blue work pants, and simple black shoes. Her usual costume.

"Sorry I'm late," I said.

"It's okay. It's quiet," she said, then she pushed her reading glasses back up her nose and went back to her Korean-language newspaper.

I took my usual seat on the other side of the waiting room, across from the desk, and fished out the novel I was reading, which was in the front left pocket of my jacket. The book was *The Great Santini*, by Pat Conroy, and it was my second time reading it—I'm a sucker sometimes for sadistic-daddy books with a military angle—and I settled in and began the long wait for trouble, which might not come.

Mrs. Pak also owned the Laundromat and the nail salon on the ground floor, and I had been doing my laundry at her place for a long time, and about a year before, when I was waiting for my clothes to dry, she asked me if I could provide security at the spa in the evenings. She knew I was an ex-cop and ran my own business, and she thought it might be a good fit. I was broke and said yes, without really thinking it through, and so I became the muscle at a jerk-off farm, which wasn't something to be proud of.

I did seven years in the Navy, ten years in the LAPD, and since 2004 I'd been on my own. Working the Thai Miracle Spa was not where I thought I'd be at fifty, but it's where I ended up, working Monday through Saturday, six to midnight.

During the day at the spa, it was a mix of female and male clients, but the night trade was different: there were almost no women customers and a lot of the men had their drink on, which was why Mrs. Pak had wanted security. The strip mall is right near the entrance to the 101 and a lot of these drunks stopped off at the spa on their way home to the Valley.

Of course the girls weren't supposed to have sex with the customers, but Mrs. Pak looked the other way at what she called "prostate release." What she didn't look the other way at was the extra cash it brought in, which she split 60/40 with the girls—60 for her, 40 for the girls. Which was much better terms than most.

It was supposed to be a Thai spa, but all the girls were from China, and it was a crew of about twenty. They worked at all three locations—the Laundromat, the nail salon, and the Miracle—and it was like a big family. Mrs. Pak's eighty-something mother cooked for everyone. In the back room of the salon, lunch was served at one, dinner at nine.

Mrs. Pak had one son—an ER doctor at Cedars-Sinai, whom she put through medical school at UCLA—but he never came around. Her ex-husband, a gambling addict and an old-fashioned morphine addict, lived in Reno, and so I was the only man on the premises, other than customers.

That night things were slow at first and I was tearing through the Conroy novel. In the Navy, they called me the Dictionary because I always had a book and liked to do cross-word puzzles.

Then around eight things began to get busy, and whenever a man came in, I stood up and gave him a look while he conducted his business with Mrs. Pak.

Once the man paid, she'd lead him through the beaded curtain on the other side of the room and then down the hallway, which had eight little massage rooms, four on each side.

The look I gave the men wasn't meant to frighten them off but to let them know that someone was there and that there were rules to follow. Loose rules. No intercourse, no oral sex, but hand jobs and a little fondling were okay. Also nursing.

Mrs. Pak had told me that a lot of the men just liked to suckle on the girls and would pay dearly for it, and I couldn't say I didn't understand. My mother died in childbirth and I was never breast-fed. Not even by a wet nurse. My analyst has implied—she doesn't say things directly—that this is a big part of my problem in life and I don't disagree.

It's also something of an issue for me that my first breath was my mother's last. It's hard to forgive yourself for something like that, and it doesn't make it easy for your father to forgive you, either, or even to love you. All of which has led to a strange life with George and four days a week on the couch. I think I'm the only ex-cop I know in Freudian analysis, but I could be wrong.

So I didn't like the rules at the spa, didn't like being complicit with what was going on, but being low on cash had made me stupid, and then I got caught up in thinking—more stupidity, *vain* stupidity—that the girls needed me.

At least three times a week, one of the drunken idiots who came for the prostate release—but then wanted something more—would get violent and rough, and I'd have to step in and do some arm-twisting, which does come natural to me. I'm six two, 190, all lean muscle from eating canned fish the way I do, and in the Navy I was a cop and in the cops I was a cop, so I know how to subdue people. There are two basic rules: bark loudly and act first.

It also helps to have a weapon, and at the spa, I carried a sixteen-inch steel telescopic baton, the kind that starts out eight inches but expands when you flick it, and it fit nicely in the large front right pocket of my blazer, which is my jacket of choice.

Every day of my life, I wear the same basic outfit: tropical-weight blue blazer, blue or tan khaki pants, and a blue or white button-down shirt. I also wear, every day, black ankle boots. They're good for kicking people, if it comes to that, and I also like the *click-clack* the wooden heels make as I walk—it's like out of a movie, the sound effect of a man in a city late at night, alone and in danger. It's a romantic sound.

At the spa, I also carried in the front pocket of my blazer a small belly gun, which I had never fired and never wanted to fire. It was there as a deterrent and as a last resort.

So I was well set up to take care of the drunks, and upon

my recommendation, Mrs. Pak had splurged on a neat little system to help me know if the girls were in trouble. There was a switch on their massage tables they could hit if things were getting out of control, and on the coffee table next to me was a little electronic board, like the kind they used to use at restaurants for seating, and if a girl in, let's say, room 6 was having trouble, a little red light—the sixth one on the panel—would start flashing.

It wasn't a foolproof system, but it was better than relying on one of the girls screaming for help—she might not get the chance, but she might get to the switch.

That night a girl screamed.

5.

MRS. PAK HAD STAYED at the desk until nine o'clock, when a girl named June replaced her. At 9:10 another girl brought us our dinner—a bowl of bibimbap: vegetables and rice with monkfish.

At 9:45, I tried the Mirage, but Lou wasn't at the front desk. The owner, Aram, a friend of mine, answered the phone and said Lou hadn't shown up for work.

"Is he in his room?"

"No, he's not in there," Aram said. "I don't know where he is. So I'm stuck working the desk and I haven't had dinner." Aram's an Armenian man in his midsixties, and we've gotten friendly over the years playing backgammon, a passion for both of us, and sometimes he's hired me to chase away drug dealers.

"When Lou turns up, tell him to call me," I said.

"Right," he said, and we hung up.

At around 10:20, a big guy came in. Real big. I stood up and felt small, which doesn't happen to me too often. This piece of meat was about six six, 340, most of it in his belly. He was wearing sweatpants and a sweatshirt and had a shaved white head the size of a watermelon made of fat. A dirty backpack was slung over his shoulder.

He had a blondish-red goatee, cauliflower ears, and small, pink-rimmed eyes, like a rat. All his features were tiny and strange, like they'd been glued onto the wrong head. Even his nose was small, just a button, and he must have gotten his deformed ears from wrestling or being in too many fights, and he looked at me with his brown rat eyes and I looked at him with my blue eyes, and he gave me the creeps. I fingered the steel baton in my pocket.

But he was polite to June, soft-spoken the way a lot of big men are, and he asked for the body wash and the salt scrub.

In room 8, there was a special shower with a long rubber hose and a waterproof massage bed. The girls would put on rain boots and a bathing suit, and it was a high-priced item. Rat Eyes gave June his credit card—all went smoothly—and then she led him through the curtain and down the hallway. A sweet girl named Mei was working room 8, and I didn't envy her the task of sluicing that big boy's nasty body.

I sat back down, picked up my book, but got distracted and thought about Monica. Why did she, out of the blue, tell me she loved me? I knew it probably just meant that she loved me as a friend and nothing more, but maybe she was also open to giving me a second chance. It had been four years since our one night, and I hadn't been with anyone since.

At 10:43, I heard the scream.

June stood up and I stood up. I ran through the beaded curtain and a couple of the girls popped out of their rooms. Where did the scream come from? The doors to rooms 3, 5, and 8 were still closed, and then there was another scream. Seemed to be coming from room 8. Which made sense.

Rat Eyes.

I took the baton out of my pocket and flicked it to its full length. I yanked the door open and Rat Eyes was on the far side of the room and had the rubber shower hose around Mei's neck. She was in her bathing suit, her eyes were bulging out of her head, and his immense body was naked and wet. He saw me and dropped Mei and dashed for his backpack, which was on a chair with his clothes. Out came a big hunting knife.

Water was all over the floor and there was a chemical smell in the air—I saw a glass pipe on the counter by the towels. He had smoked some meth and was out of his mind.

He charged me like a wet bull and I flashed to his orange pubes. Same color as my father's, and the purple head of his penis was poking out of the pubes like some kind of hideous growth, and all of it was tucked under the slick monstrous slab of his stomach.

The whole thing threw me—my father's Irish pubes, Mei lying dead or unconscious on the floor, water everywhere, Rat Eyes's cock—and I was slow to react. I didn't bark and I didn't go first, and he was on me and slicing down at me with the knife and I got my left forearm up just in time and took the blow there, the knife cutting through my jacket and deep into my skin.

As I was blocking him, I took a swing at his rib cage with the baton, but I was all off balance and it was a weak blow and he hardly felt it, there was too much beef on him, and then he was slicing down at me again and this time his blow was stronger and it knocked my arm out of the way and the blade caught my face and sliced my cheek open and I could feel it peel off like a sticker.

Then suddenly we were on the floor—he had slipped and brought me with him—and the back of my head bounced off the hard tile and I lost the baton, and he climbed on top of me, naked and slippery, and the knife was in the air and then coming down at me, to stab me, and my eyes were filled with blood from my cheek, but I was able to grab his wrist with my left hand and I made my right hand like a knife, my fingers all together, like they teach you in self-defense, and you either go for the eyes or the throat, and I jabbed him hard in the left eye, and that got through the meth and he screamed and rolled off of me, and I rolled away, and then we were both trying to stand on the slippery floor, and he was squinting, and I got to my feet first and kicked him in the shoulder, which didn't do much, and on his knees he swiped at me with his knife and nearly got me, and so then I took out my belly gun and meant to shoot him in the leg to slow him down, but my hand was unsteady, and I shot him through the neck and blood geysered out in a spray.

And when he toppled over, Mei sat up, like it was choreographed, like they were puppets, one dead, one alive, and then I sat down, like a yogi, in the blood pooling around his body. I think I was in shock: I had never killed a man before, and the girls were crowding the door to the room, and I turned to look at them and could feel something tickling my neck. It was the flap of my face. I tried to put it back in place and one of the girls screamed.

I said, all calm and relaxed and in shock: "Has anyone called 911?"

6.

AFTER THE COPS ARRIVED, Mrs. Pak called her son and he pulled strings and the EMTs brought me to Cedars-Sinai instead of the Presbyterian hospital on Vermont, which was closer.

Mei wasn't injured, just badly shaken up, so she stayed with Mrs. Pak and her mother. Her son, Dr. Pak, met my ambulance in the driveway outside the ER at Cedars, escorted me inside, and had already arranged for a top plastic surgeon to put my face back on.

Before I went into surgery, I called Monica at the Dresden and told her what had happened, without getting too gory, and she said she'd get George and take him back to her place. She knew where I hid my key.

And before she hung up, she said it again: "You know, I love you, Hap."

I got thirty stitches in my arm and thirty in my face—nice and symmetrical. The good news—not that I really cared at that time—was that with both cuts the blade hadn't gone too deep and there was minimal nerve damage.

In the morning, Dr. Pak came to see me—my face was heavily bandaged—and he switched my pain meds, unsolicited, to the good stuff: Dilaudid. He explained to me that the face has a lot of nerves and I should anticipate a fair amount of pain, but that the meds should get me through it. He also told me that his mother would pick up any additional expenses that my insurance wouldn't cover, and I didn't say no.

After he left, I did feel a little embarrassed that I hadn't offered any kind of protest to this offer of financial assistance, but my pride was as thin as my bank account. I had no savings and my only asset was my house, and the only reason it was paid off was because it was willed to me in 2011 by a client, Mrs. Rubenstein, after she died.

I had come to know her because for a long time most of my work as a private investigator had been for the elderly. When I first hung out my shingle, I got hooked up with a gerontologist, a Dr. Schine, who sent me a lot of his patients. Senior citizens are ripe for all sorts of scams and it became kind of a niche market for me, albeit a small one.

Then in 2017, Dr. Schine, sadly and ironically, got hit with early-onset dementia, retired, and closed his practice. Overnight he went from caring for old people to being one—it was strange karma—and without him feeding me work, I slowly went broke and ended up at the Miracle.

But long before all that happened, Dr. Schine sent me Mrs. Fanny Rubenstein, a ninety-year-old Austrian émigré, a retired violin teacher who had been married to a violin *maker,* Irving Rubenstein.

Irving was from a long line of Viennese violin makers, and when Hitler annexed Austria, in '38, Mr. Rubenstein—they were living in Vienna at the time—took a big risk and mailed a precious violin that had been in the family for several generations to a cousin in America for safekeeping.

The cousin, a costume designer, was in the movie business in Los Angeles.

So they sent their violin to California, and they sent their little girl, six years old, to relatives in France who lived in Lyon. They didn't want their child too far away, and no one thought then that France would fall so easily, or fall at all.

In 1940, Mr. and Mrs. Rubenstein got carted off to Buchenwald but somehow survived. Their daughter and their relatives in Lyon didn't.

Then in 1950, after a few years in Israel, the Rubensteins came to Los Angeles, got the violin, and made a new life on Glen Alder Street, where they bought, on the side of the hill, my little bungalow, which they named after their daughter, Frimma, the little girl they had sent to France and never saw again.

They had forty years together on Glen Alder—he made and repaired violins, and she taught—and then Irving died in the early '90s. After he passed, Mrs. Rubenstein withdrew from the world, stopped teaching, and became a recluse. Then in 2011, her home health aide figured out that the old violin, hidden in a special humidor in the linen closet, was worth something, and so she quit her job, took the thing, and tried to sell it.

Mrs. Rubenstein told Dr. Schine what had happened and then he told me, and without too much effort, I was able to get the violin back. Then Mrs. Rubenstein gave it to the LA Phil—it was called a Guarneri and the Phil sold it to the Louvre for four million. All of which, Mrs. Rubenstein said, would have pleased her husband very much. They had gone to the LA Phil for decades, and it was Irving's passion.

A few months after the sale to the Louvre, Mrs. Rubenstein died and left me the house on Glen Alder—left me Frimma—as a way to thank me.

7.

AROUND TWO P.M., a nurse—a sweet gal named Nancy—came to take more blood. I looked away because I'm squeamish, and then I had a eureka moment of sorts.

"What's my blood type?" I asked her, excited. That is, as excited as you can get when you're on Dilaudid, just got thirty stitches in your face, and have killed a man.

Florence told me it was O positive, and when she was done drawing my blood I asked for my phone. She found it in the closet—where they were also keeping my blood-soaked clothes in a plastic bag—and it had only 3 percent battery. I realized that something must be draining the phone more than usual, some app or something, when I wasn't using the damn thing, but I didn't have the slightest idea how to go about fixing it.

There were several texts and missed calls from Monica. She wanted to know if she could come see me and was I okay? There was also a voice mail from my analyst, Dr. Lavich, wondering where I was that morning. I certainly had a reasonable excuse, but I had completely forgotten about our morning session and it had never occurred to me to call her. This would have to be discussed in our next session, along with other pressing headlines, like what had happened last night at the spa.

In the meantime, I left her a brief message on her answering machine: "Dr. Lavich, it's Hank—Happy—Doll. I'm so sorry I missed today's session. Something unexpected happened. Will fill you in when I see you. I also can't make it tomorrow morning, but I'll be there Friday." I had analysis four times a week, Tuesday through Friday, at nine a.m.

Then I texted Monica that I was fine and that today I needed to rest, but that maybe tomorrow, when they let me out, she could come get me with some clothes. I didn't mention that all my clothes in the plastic bag in the closet were covered in blood. And most of it not mine.

There were no missed calls or voice mails from Lou, and before the phone died I tried his number and got the answering machine again. I left another message: "Lou, it's Hank. Where are you? Listen—ran into some trouble at the spa. Got cut bad. And the other guy... well, I'll tell you when I see you. I'm at Cedars-Sinai. The good news is that I'm O positive, which means we're a go on the kidney. Call me back."

Then I tried the front desk of the Mirage, spoke to Aram again, and asked if he'd seen or heard from Lou. He hadn't and was getting worried.

I said: "He'll turn up soon," and we hung up, and there was a pinprick of fear at the back of my neck, wondering what Lou was up to, but I shrugged it off and it quickly subsided in the warm bath of the painkiller. Then I asked Nancy, who was hovering, messing with my chart and my tube of blood, if she could charge my phone.

She said yes, started to leave with it, then turned at the door and said, "Would it be okay if I asked you something?"

"Sure," I said.

"Is your name really Happy Doll?"

I took a breath and said, "Yeah, Happy Doll, that's me," and I gave her a sad-clown smile, and she nodded, looked embarrassed now that she had asked the question, which hadn't been my intention, and left the room.

I fell asleep again for about an hour, and then two homicide detectives paid me a visit. One was fat and one was skinny.

The fat one said: "Can you talk?" He indicated my bandages.

"Yeah."

"I'm Mullen," said the fat cop, who had a fringe of hair around his bald head, and then he jerked his thumb at his partner. "This is Thode."

Thode smiled at me, but it was a nasty smile. His lips were sensuous and purple, and he had dark, pretty eyelashes, but his eyes were unkind. He'd seen the worst in people and *thought* the worst of people. Being a cop had made him that way; it had done other things to me.

"So you know the drill," said Mullen, breathing hard because of his weight. His round face was red and his eyes were red; his whole body was aggrieved. "Tell us what happened. And try not to lie."

I didn't understand his attitude or the way Thode was looking at me. But I shrugged it all off—maybe the Dilaudid was making me read things the wrong way—and I kept it simple. I said: "The guy went berserk. He was on meth and threatening one of the girls, and I got my face carved. Had to put him down."

"Don't be an asshole," said Thode. He took out his notepad; he was the stenographer of the pair. "We gotta see if your story matches the girl's. Now tell it. In detail." More attitude. So I gave some back:

"Well, I was sitting in the front, reading a really good book," and I said this in a singsong kind of voice to annoy them, but Mullen cut me off before I could go any further.

"Quit fooling around," he snapped. "And why the fuck were you working there in the first place? You should be ashamed. You were a cop once. You make us all look bad."

Now I understood their animosity: they saw me as a cautionary tale, what life might be like after the badge, and it scared them. You ended up working at a spa. Fine—let them be scared.

"You want my story or not?" I rasped; my throat was dry.

"Go ahead," said Thode.

I looked at them and then I launched into it: "So I'm sitting there—*reading a really good book*—and I hear a scream. I run to the back and there's another scream. Room 8. I go in and he's strangling the girl with the shower hose. I had my baton out and he grabs a big hunting knife out of his bag. I don't know why he had that knife—but he must have been planning something; maybe he was going to cut the girl—and he had been smoking meth and was going haywire. I got in one whack with the baton, but he was a bull and cut me twice and then brought me down. I managed to get him off me, but he was still swinging the knife and I shot him." I left out the part about not meaning to kill him. Didn't think that would win their favor one way or the other.

"Do you know who you killed?" said Thode.

"A meth head."

"Not exactly, asshole," he said. "His name was Carl Lusk. Played for USC ten years ago. Was going to the NFL but blew out his knee senior year. Drug problems since and a couple of arrests for assault and solicitation." Then he blinked his girly eyelashes twice even though he didn't mean to; he was a twitcher.

"So why are you coming down on me?" I said. "Okay, he's an ex–football star, but he's also a felon and he would have killed that girl." I had never heard of Lusk.

"He's not just an ex–football star," said Mullen. "His dad's a cop. We know him. Bill Lusk. Works downtown. Also Homicide."

Now their attitudes were really starting to make sense: I was a cautionary tale *and* I'd killed the son of one of their friends, a fellow cop, though I'd never heard of the father, either. I had worked the Missing Persons Unit in Hollywood for the bulk of my years on the force, specifically, the juvie division: runaways, homeless teens, stolen children. But that ended a long time ago and I had never crossed paths with a detective named Lusk.

"I don't know him," I said, "and I wish I hadn't shot his son, but that football star was big, and if he got through me, he was going to kill one of those girls, maybe all of them. Why'd he have that knife? Not for protection."

"Bullshit," said Mullen, his eyes angry in his round face. "You snapped. We asked around about you. They said you were weird and cracked at the end of your tour. Is that what happened last night? You couldn't just put Lusk down? We found your little wand." He pantomimed a swing with the baton. "You had to kill him? Really?"

"I tried to put him down. Couldn't. He was too big. He nearly cut my face off."

"He was naked," said Thode. "Should have been easy. I think you panicked."

I didn't have anything to say to that. There was no talking to these two, and they made a few threats about the DA and possible manslaughter charges and I didn't really care. The Dilaudid had me feeling far, far away, *and* I had killed a man. No matter what they threatened, I couldn't get any lower.

When they finally left me alone, I tried to sleep but it wasn't possible: I kept seeing Rat Eyes—Carl Lusk—coming at me. The knife raised. The knife coming down.

8.

MONICA CAME FOR ME around noon the next day, Thursday, and she brought me some fresh clothes, picked up at my house, to change into. I was given a printout of "wound-care" instructions and a prescription for more Dilaudid, which I was becoming quite fond of.

I had a big white square bandage on my face, anchored by several horizontal strips of tape that went across my nose, and my arm was also trussed up.

They wheeled me to the front door—protocol—and then I stood up and walked out of the hospital and my legs were a little wobbly, but it was good to be outside. It was bright and chilly and there was a strong wind. It was the best winter in LA in years: lots of rain and cold, and when the sun was out, like it was then, the light was crystalline and pure.

When we got in her car, a dirty black Prius, she said: "Did you see the *LA Times*?"

"No. Is it bad? I haven't wanted to look at my phone."

"Front page," she said. "The tragic story of a football player. There were a lot of quotes from the coach. But your name doesn't come up until later in the paper. I don't think people will read that far."

I nodded. Then: "What does it say about me?"

"They said it was self-defense. That you saved the girl."

I lowered my head. If only I could have saved her without pulling my gun. Then Monica, trying to lighten things up, pointed at my bandage: "You know, we're gonna be twins now. Scars on the left side."

And she traced her finger down her scar: the thin pink line that ran from just below her eye to her jawline. It was like she had cried so much one time that a path had been cut, like a riverbed.

"Yeah, we'll match," I said, trying to be light, too. "They're gonna love it at the bar."

Except it wasn't light. Monica got her scar when her father, drunk, pushed her through a plate-glass window. She was six years old, and he went to jail for it and she never saw him again. When he got out, he disappeared, and she talked sometimes about finding him. She had heard once that he was in Ecuador, where he was from.

We made a quick stop at the pharmacy for my drugs, and then when she pulled up in front of Glen Alder, she turned off the Prius and wanted to help me up the stairs.

"I'm fine," I said. "I can manage. But thanks for getting me...and for George, and for everything." George was already inside; Monica had dropped him off before coming to the hospital.

"Of course," she said, and then we hugged in the front seat and when I tried to pull away, she held on tight, wouldn't let go, and so I exhaled and gave over to some deep need and put the right side of my face—my good side now—into her neck and her hair, and it felt so good. I hadn't been that close to anyone since our night four years ago, and I wondered how I could have gone so long without this feeling.

Then she began to let go of me, and we parted and looked at each other and she smiled, and I looked away, suddenly shy, and became aware that outside the windshield, we were surrounded by hundreds of fluttering orange-and-black butterflies. They were flying courageously but somewhat spasmodically in the wind.

"What's going on?" I said to Monica.

"It's the Painted Ladies," she said. "Started yesterday. They keep appearing all over the place. Flocks of them. Because of all the rain and climate change there are millions of them this year."

"It's beautiful," I said.

"I know," she said. "Like flowers that can fly."

We sat there and looked at them. Then I opened the door and started to slide out, but Monica touched my arm, stopping me. "Don't do that again," she said. "No more fights."

Then she kissed my good cheek and restarted the car. I slid all the way out and then lowered my head into the still-open door. My bag of bloody clothes was in my hand.

"Thank you again," I said. "For taking care of George. For picking me up—"

She cut me off. "You already said that and you don't have to thank me. I love you."

Then I said, "I love *you*," without hesitation or fear, and she smiled wide and her eyes twinkled like they do, and I closed the door. She pulled away, and my heart was pounding. I had given up on love.

Then I climbed the stairs to my house, and I greeted Frimma and the plants and the trees. "Hello, everyone," I said. "I'm home. You're all looking so beautiful."

And from inside the house, George barked his greeting, and the Painted Ladies, like auguries of good things, I thought, fluttered around me.

9.

WHILE MONICA AND I had been sitting in the car, Lou finally called me back—my ringer was off—and left a message. He sounded exuberant. He said:

"What happened, Hank? Somebody cut you? But listen, I got everything worked out! Some things came through and I won't need your help after all. But thank you, son, for being willing. That means a lot. I'll call you later. I got things to do. Hope you're not cut too bad."

I wondered what things had come through. Someone else was going to give him a kidney? I listened to the message again. He had never called me son before, and he didn't say anything about where he had been since Tuesday.

I tried him back but got the damn machine again. I didn't bother leaving a message this time, and my face was starting to throb bad, so I took a Dilaudid and crawled into bed with George.

I slept for more than six hours and woke up around nine. I got dressed and thought of getting an Uber and retrieving my Caprice, which was still at the spa, but I decided I was too loopy from the pill and took another one. Dilaudid, they say, is the closest there is to heroin. Makes Oxycontin look like a weak sister.

Feeling a little hungry, but not too much, because of the pill, I had a can of lentil soup and some pickles. My usual dinner. Then I ate a marijuana gummy for dessert, thinking it would mix nice with the Dilaudid. I made the mistake of checking my phone, which was nearly dead again, and there were a number of missed calls and text messages. Much more than usual. People must have seen the article in the paper. I didn't listen to any of the voice mails or read any of the texts, and I didn't bother to charge the thing.

Stoned, I watched a Lakers game, and all the while images of me shooting Lusk hovered on the edge of my consciousness, like this thing I should be attending to, but I kept pushing it out of my mind.

Then after the Lakers game, I went to the bathroom to look at myself, which I had managed not to do at the hospital.

I removed my bandage, and even on the drugs, I nearly swooned. The skin was all purple and green and yellow, and the black stitches formed a hideous pucker down the middle of my cheek, like a raised seam on a baseball glove.

I quickly put the bandage back on, and there in the mirror were my father's blue eyes and my mother's black hair, cut short; my busted big nose and my chin with stubble. But I didn't seem to know this guy and I didn't like him.

I said to the face: *What did you do? You killed a man.*

I know, the face said. *But he was going to kill Mei, and he was suicidal. He used me to die.*

George, hearing me talk to someone, came into the bathroom, and I felt a little more sane. "George, I killed a man," I said.

He looked at me with compassion, and so then I treated

myself to half a Dilaudid and half a marijuana gummy and took George for a walk. Glen Alder is a dead-end street with a cul-de-sac—which is where my house is, on the right side of the cul-de-sac—and we went down to Beachwood and up to Glen Holly, our usual route.

Back at the house, I grabbed a blanket and we lay down on the couch I have on the side porch, which is on the other side of the house from George's little chicken coop. I hooked George up to the lead I keep on the porch—otherwise he'd dash off into the woods after skunks and coyotes—and he lay on my chest, under the blanket, with his face poking out and resting by my chin, and together we listened to the night birds and the night wind and the far-off sounds of the city: sirens and traffic rumble and revving motorcycles.

And in the sky the full moon was unusually large and beautiful.

At two a.m. I woke up. I was still high as hell and George was barking and I realized he'd been barking for a while. Someone was banging at the front door. I unhooked George and we went back into the house. I opened the front door and it was Lou.

He smiled weakly at me and then did a half twist and fell into my arms.

I pulled him inside and dragged him to the couch in the living room. I lay him down and his raincoat flopped open and the front of his white shirt was red with blood.

"Got shot," he whispered.

His right hand flopped to the floor and George started licking the blood off it.

"George," I shouted, and I pushed him away and opened up Lou's shirt. There was a black puncture, a hole about the size of a nickel, and dark-red blood was oozing out of it. I took Lou's hand and put it over the hole.

"Keep pressure on it!" I said, then ran into the kitchen, where my phone was, and it was dead! "Goddamn it!" I screamed.

I nearly lost control and threw the thing against the wall, but I had sense enough not to. I cursed myself for not having a landline, and I plugged the phone in, grabbed a dish towel, and ran back to Lou. My panic was rubbery. The Dilaudid and the marijuana had me all messed up, like the volume inside me was set much too loud. I knew I had to keep my head, but my head was gone.

Lou's eyes were closed and his blood-smeared hand had flopped back to the floor, and George was licking it again. I pushed George away and knelt next to Lou and applied pressure to the hole in his belly with the dish towel.

I said: "I'm going to call 911 in a second, Lou. Just have to charge the damn fucking phone."

His eyes opened. He looked at me sideways. He whispered: "I don't think it matters."

I ignored that and said: "Who shot you, Lou? What happened?"

"Don't know their names. That was the deal. But I got the one who got me." He seemed to smile and he was going to say something else, but a vicious pain shot through him and he bared his little yellow teeth, and then he exhaled and closed his eyes and his face smoothed out.

I thought maybe he had died—he didn't seem to be breathing—and I dug a finger into his neck and didn't feel a pulse, but then he opened his eyes again and shoved his bloody hand into the pocket of his raincoat and came out with a folded square of blue paper, now smeared with blood.

"For my daughter," he whispered, passing me the blue square. "Worth a lot more than I thought. Sell it for her, get the money—"

Then suddenly his head went back unnaturally and the crown of his skull dug into the back of the couch, like he was trying to get away from something, and then as quick as that happened, he suddenly went still, much too still, and I could smell wretched feces, and then his head relaxed and fell to the side, like a bird with a broken neck, and Lou Shelton was dead.

Like I said, he was a hard man to kill.

Until he wasn't.

PART II

1.

I WAS KNEELING by the couch and my hand was still pressed against the wound.

We'd been like that for a while. Several minutes at least. Lou was dead but hadn't left my house, and there was a lull in the noise in my head, a deep silence.

But then George started barking loudly and broke the spell. I thought maybe he was barking because Lou had died, and I turned and said, "George!"

But George was facing the door. That meant he was barking at something outside. I stood up and looked out the window and there was a man paused midway up the stairs, hesitating to come forward because of the barking, and there was a gun in his hand down by his thigh. I could see him clearly in the moonlight, and he saw me in the window.

He was wearing a Dodgers baseball hat pulled low, obscuring his face, but he was tall and wide, and he raised his gun—it looked like a .22 and Lou was likely shot with a .22; the wound in his gut had been small but lethal—and I ducked down and flipped off the light, which had framed me in the window like a target.

But no bullet came crashing through the glass, which would have alerted the neighbors and probably not killed me. A .22 is good for close-in work, execution work. So the man had been smart not to fire, and I peeked out the window, and he was running, in a controlled way, back down the stairs to the fence and the gate. He had lost the element of surprise—I could be armed for all he knew—and he was retreating, like a professional. He had raised the gun as a feint, a way to buy himself time to get away.

I whipped the front door open and went flying after him in my socks, but there's too many damn stairs, and as I got to the street, a black Land Rover was already halfway down the block, and it had dealer plates, which made it useless to trace. Lou's car, an old yellow Maverick, was parked haphazardly by the curb.

"Fuck," I said, and I started to run up the stairs, thinking I'd get in my car and chase the Land Rover—it would go either left or right on Beachwood and maybe I could catch it.

But as I got inside, I remembered, cursing myself, that my car, which I had been too lazy to get, was still at the spa, and so then I went like a madman to Lou's body to get his keys and started frantically rifling around in his pockets, taking far too long, and, of course, the last thing I actually found were his keys, and by then I knew there was no chance of catching anybody. But Lou's pockets, amid a bunch of crap—coins, tissues, lighters, matches, cigarettes, lottery tickets, chewing gum—*did* turn up three things of interest:

His gun. A 9mm Glock: with nine bullets in the clip, one missing.

A train ticket stub: a return trip to LA from Carlsbad that morning.

And a little blue spiral notebook with the binding at the top: the kind cops and reporters used to use, back in the day, which Lou still carried all the time for phone numbers and to-do lists, addresses, and other miscellany.

The cover was flipped back to the last page Lou had written on, and there in his chicken scratch was a list of what looked to be departure or arrival times, which jibed with the ticket stub, and two addresses: 550 Hill Street, suite 834, which was a downtown address, and 2803 Belden Drive, which was about a mile from my house.

Reading that second address gave me a jolt. Is that where Lou had just come from? Is that where he was shot? It made sense: he couldn't have gone too far with that bullet in his gut, and I was nearby, so he came to me, and the tall man in the Dodgers hat must have followed him from there. But what had Lou been doing on Belden?

Then I remembered the square piece of blue paper, which I had shoved into my pocket when George started barking. I got the thing out and unfolded the paper and in the center of it was a fat rectangular diamond, about half an inch long. It gleamed in my palm. Like money.

Like something you might get killed for.

I rewrapped it and shoved it back in my pocket. Then I took Lou's car keys and gun—mine had been confiscated at the spa—and started to run out to go to 2803 Belden to see what I could find. Maybe Dodgers Hat had gone back there. And I was halfway down the steps when I realized I still didn't have any shoes on.

How fucking high am I? I wondered, and it was like I was operating on two planes. Screwing up. And watching myself screw up.

What I should have been doing—the sane thing to do—was call the cops and put all of Lou's stuff, especially the gun, back in his pockets, but instead I ran up the stairs to my bedroom, threw on a jacket, got my shoes, and came back down.

George was licking Lou's fingers again and I shooed him away. Then I threw the blanket from the porch over Lou's body, got his hand off the floor and tucked it under the blanket, and said to George, "Leave Lou alone."

Then I was out of there, down the stairs, and Lou's car reeked like an ashtray and the old engine coughed twice—like a smoker, like Lou—before turning over, and in two minutes, after speeding north on Beachwood, I was climbing Belden Drive, which went straight up the canyon. Near the very top, 2803 stood alone on the right-hand side of an S curve, high above a culvert.

I slowed the Maverick down, and the house was a long rectangular white box, set back just a few feet from the street, with an attached garage and a tall hedge that shrouded the entrance in privacy. In the glaring moonlight, the whiteness of the house seemed to glow.

Across the way, on the left-hand side, was a large Spanish house elevated high above the road, on the side of the hill, and that house was dark, as was 2803. There were no other neighbors on this twisted bit of road and no cars parked on the street, no Land Rovers.

I kept on going and stashed Lou's car about a hundred yards away, around another curve, where some houses had clustered, lined up along the cliff's edge.

Then I walked back toward the house.

My hand was in my pocket, on Lou's gun, and it was very quiet up there at the top of the mountain—it was like a narrow country road, trees everywhere—and my shoes made that movie sound of a man walking on pavement.

But aware that my *click-clacking* heels could be a liability, I began to walk quietly as I approached 2803, which was now on my left. No cars were coming or could be seen down below, and there were no streetlights up here, but the world was perfectly visible with the full moon like a white sun, and because of the marijuana and the Dilaudid, it all seemed to be extra luminous and even vibrational.

I passed the hedges near the entrance to take a look at the garage. There were leaves piled up where the garage door met the pavement, and so it didn't seem likely that the Land Rover or any other car was parked inside. Those leaves, blown by the wind, had been there awhile.

Gun out in front of me, I then went through the portal cut into the hedges, and leaning against the house—hidden from the street—was a weather-beaten FOR SALE sign, the kind where the agent has included a picture, like an actor's head shot. The realty company was called Ken Maurais, and the air-brushed agent—who had feathered-back frosted hair and fake teeth and was giving a look meant to inspire trust but which did the opposite—was also someone named Ken Maurais.

He must have been a one-man operation, and I stared at his picture for a second, and then I crouched below the front window and crab-walked my way to the edge of the house. When the wall came to an end, there was a deep, vertiginous drop into the culvert below.

So this was one of those places, when seen from the street, you think is just a single-story ranch house, but get past its hedges and you realize the "ground floor" is actually the pent-house and that the building goes down and down and down, a vertical mansion built against the side of a hill, with no land to speak of.

I crouched back under the window and went to the front door. On my house-key chain there's a small but powerful Maglite and a little doohickey that's good for opening locks, but that wasn't necessary. The door was already open a crack, and using my foot, I eased it open farther and went in, with Lou's gun leading the way.

The room I entered was devoid of furniture and was well lit by the moon, and the impression, as you stepped in, was of being high on a cliff in a special glass box. Across from the entrance, twenty feet away, was an enormous picture window, which could slide open like a glass door, and it was nearly as wide as the whole house, and beyond that was a balcony and beyond the balcony was a dazzling rich man's view: the dark canyon with its scattered house lights, like a hillside in Italy, and then in the distance, the skyline of downtown LA, a jagged crown of light.

It was mesmerizing and you could see for miles.

But up close there was also something to see. A dead man. A little to my right, he was on the floor, laid out flat on his back. I walked over to the body and there was a black hole in the middle of his forehead. I nudged the body with my foot. It was my second dead man of the night and third in two days. I was getting jaded.

He was a blonde kid, midtwenties, handsome, except for the black hole bored into his skull. And I wondered if that hole had been caused by the missing round in Lou's gun, which was now the gun in *my* hand, getting covered in *my* prints.

I checked the blonde's pockets, but they were empty—no wallet, no cell phone, no keys, no gun. He'd been stripped.

The floor was a pale wood, and there was a vivid trail of blood that started at his head and went to the right, down a short hallway. It seemed like someone had grabbed him by the ankles and pulled him along the floor toward the front door. The leaking wound in the back of his head—matching the hole in the front of his head—had left a smear, and I followed the blood trail down the hallway to a narrow elevator door, where the blood trail ended.

I stopped and listened a moment. Had I heard something? Was anyone else here? I went back out to the empty room, but there was no one there and no one on the balcony, just a rusted cooking grill. I stood quietly, hardly breathing, but didn't hear anything and decided to keep exploring. I needed to understand what had happened to Lou.

I went back to the elevator, pushed the button, and the door opened. The narrow compartment lit up and there was blood on the elevator floor, continuing the blood trail from the hallway. I stepped into the elevator, to the side of the blood, and in the corner there was a bullet shell, which I picked up and looked at. It matched the bullets in Lou's gun.

Let's touch all the evidence, I said to myself, and pocketed the thing. At some point soon, I was going to have a lot of explaining to do. But I was putting it off. I seemed to know only one direction: forward.

Recklessly forward.

I was on 6 and pushed the buttons for all the floors, 5 through 1.

At each floor, the door opened, but there was no blood trail until the bottom floor, where it picked up again and led to the far left side of a table, which was across from the elevator. There were five folding chairs around the table and a water glass in front of each chair, with a Pellegrino bottle in the middle. Some kind of meeting had happened here, and there was no other furniture in the room.

In the corner was a sliding glass door, which the moonlight was coming through, lighting everything like an X-ray. I slid the door open and stepped outside onto a concrete patio about half the size of a basketball court. This was the bottom of the steep culvert, and there were a few pieces of metal patio furniture lying about, just their skeletons, no cushions, all of it rusted. Craning my neck, I looked to the top of the house, all six stories. You really did need an elevator.

I went back inside and looked at the blood trail some more. Someone had dragged blondie from the table to the elevator and up to the sixth floor, and then for some reason had left him there and taken off.

Or, alternatively, that person was somewhere inside, hiding, and not making themselves known.

So I had a dilemma: Should I search the whole house? Or should I go home immediately and call the cops and tell them everything? Every stupid thing I had done?

I decided to search the house.

On the first level, in addition to the denlike room with the table, there were three other empty rooms and an empty bathroom, and I got out the Maglite and nobody was hiding in the closets.

I went back to the elevator and this time I noticed that on the far wall of the compartment there was a bullet hole, but not that big. Like a .22. The hole in Lou's belly hadn't been that big, either. And Dodgers Hat had been carrying what looked like a .22. Did he kill Lou? But Lou said he got the one who got him, so it was probably blondie who had shot him. And maybe Dodgers Hat was carrying blondie's gun when he came to my house.

Then I went to the second floor, and as I searched around—more empty rooms and closets—I started seeing in my stoned mind how it might have gone down:

Lou's in the elevator and blondie is on the other side of the table.

For some reason, blondie shoots at Lou twice and hits him once before Lou can get a shot off. And blondie would've had to fire first since Lou's shot was a kill shot and blondie wouldn't have been snapping off any rounds after taking one in the head.

So blondie fires twice, and then Lou, in the elevator, fires back and kills blondie. Then the elevator door closes, and Lou is gone, and then Dodgers Hat and whoever else was at that meeting—and there were probably three others, judging by the water glasses—would have had to run up six flights to catch up to Lou, which gives him a head start.

But not enough of a head start, not with the winding roads, and so Dodgers Hat follows him straight to my place, but Lou doesn't know it. He's taken a gut shot and not thinking good.

But who was I to judge about not thinking good?

I searched the rest of the house but found no one and nothing of interest: the place was empty and hadn't been lived in for a long time.

The whole thing took me about fifteen minutes, and back on the sixth floor, I looked again at the corpse: he was a good-size boy, maybe six feet, 180, an athlete, and he was wearing a nice leather jacket and good shoes. He looked rich, well fed. Was he there to buy Lou's diamond? Was that the purpose of the meeting?

Then I went out to the balcony to think a second, to formulate the story I was going to tell the cops to explain my behavior, and I leaned against the railing and looked out at the view. Directly to the east was the Griffith Observatory, and at night, lit from within, it looked like a skull with a candle inside, and I was high above Los Angeles, like a king or a hawk, and then there was a metal screeching sound behind me, and I started to turn and something slammed into me hard, tackling me.

It was a man trying to drive me over the railing, and his head was buried in my shoulder, and all I could do was wrap my arms around him and pull him in close to negate his leverage, and I was fighting, instinctively, not to go over—to not let the railing be a fulcrum in the middle of my back—and the stitches in my arm and in my face felt like they were going to burst from the strain.

Then the man lifted his head from my shoulder and we looked at each other and it was blondie, and my adrenaline spiked, fueled by terror, and I had the greatest surge of strength in my life, and I lifted blondie, all six feet of him, all 180 pounds of him, and tossed him off the balcony, and he didn't have time to scream, and he hit one of the pieces of metal furniture, bounced off it in the moonlight, seemed to shudder, and then went still. Heaving, I stared down at him, and there was a roar in my head that lasted awhile and then there was silence, like when Lou had died.

Then, moving very slowly, in shock, I turned and went back into the house, and blondie was still on the floor with a bullet hole still in his head.

My legs buckled, but I quickly righted myself and ran down the six flights and went out to the patio, and the thing that had been a man had landed on its belly, and his head was on its side. The neck was at a disturbing angle, but the face somehow hadn't been damaged on the metal lounge chair.

I took out the Maglite and looked closely at the man on the ground. It wasn't blondie but another blonde. Only darker blonde and older. The drugs and fear had made me see things, and I leaned over, put my hands on my knees, and took some deep breaths.

Get your shit together, Hapless, I said to myself.

Hapless was what my father had called me for the first eighteen years of my life, and it only stopped when he died. And the way I had said *Hapless* in my mind was exactly how he used to say it, full of contempt, and hearing his voice in my head sobered me up a little—just a little—and I took another look at the corpse:

This blonde was dressed in expensive jeans and a light ski jacket. He was as big as the other one—at least that part I hadn't hallucinated—and he had the same aura of richness and privilege. The quality of the skin, the haircut. The handsomeness, even in death.

I searched the body and found house keys and a fob to a BMW, a silver money clip with about five hundred in cash and the initials PM embossed on it, and what looked like a burner phone with a security code. I couldn't get in the phone.

Then I pocketed all of this for my powwow with the cops. I had all sorts of things to show them now. Like three dead bodies.

2.

I TOOK THE ELEVATOR back up, and on the top floor, I went out to the balcony to try to figure out where the second blonde had come from.

In the far left-hand corner, opposite from where I had been standing, was the old rusted cooking grill, and it was mostly flush with the railing, but the end had been pushed out, and it hadn't been like that before.

Earlier it had appeared to be even with the railing, but there actually had been just enough space for the second blonde to squeeze behind it and be completely hidden, and that screeching sound I'd heard was him moving the grill out of the way when he decided to make his move. He probably had been hiding there the whole time I was in the house. I'd gotten lucky.

I left the front door open as I had found it, moved quickly through the hedges, and walked back up the desolate road to the Maverick, rehearsing my speech to the cops: "I was all fucked up on pain pills and marijuana and then my friend shows up and dies, and I can't explain it—I lost my head and went after this guy in a Dodgers hat with a gun. I guess I was trying to play the hero..."

It sounded bad, and I got in Lou's car and noticed some-thing I hadn't before. On the passenger seat, along with a lot of newspapers and sandwich wrappers and empty coffee cups—Lou wasn't a neat person—was a brochure of some kind with a picture of a diamond on the front and the letters GIA in caps.

Inside the brochure, on the first page, was Lou's name and address at the top, and below that was a diagram of a diamond, which was rectangular, like the one in the folded square of blue paper. And below the diagram was a heading—DIAMOND GRADING REPORT—and down a line was a series of words like *carat weight, color, clarity, depth, girdle, shape,* and *fluorescence,* all followed by letters and numbers, grades or codes of some kind.

There were also numeric measurements and other verbiage that was specific, I imagined, to the world of jewels. The diamond's "shape" was listed as an "emerald cut," and the one thing I could understand clearly was that Lou's diamond was a big one: seven carats.

And this brochure/grading report listed a Carlsbad address, 5345 Armada Drive, and Lou had that train ticket from Carlsbad. Maybe that's where he had been when he didn't show up for work, and so however it tied into everything, this report was more evidence, and I shoved it in my jacket pocket, got the car started, and began to drive back down the hill.

A minute later there was a ding: it was a text message on the burner phone. I had left my phone charging at the house. I put my foot on the brake just before a curve and pulled the cell phone out of my pocket. Even though the phone was locked, it showed the text on the screen. It had come in at 2:51 a.m., the current time, and was from a number without a name, 818-678-5564, and it said, in all caps:

ALL DONE. ALMOST BACK. BE READY TO GO.

I then eased my foot off the brake, thinking I should turn around. The text seemed to indicate that someone—Dodgers Hat?—was coming back to the house. But the road was too curvy and narrow. Wasn't a good spot for a U-turn.

So I was going to have to go farther down the road to turn around, but then there were headlights coming at me, from the blind side of the curve, and I had to pull over to let the car pass—there was only room for one car—and it was the Land Rover coming out of the turn! Dodgers Hat was in the passenger seat and lit by my headlights, I got more of his features: a jutting, protruding chin and a grotesque underbite. And the driver was an older gray-haired man with a large head craned forward like a vulture.

They were a hideous pair, and as the Land Rover squeezed past me, slowly, intimately, Dodgers Hat looked over and saw me, and there was recognition. He had seen me clearly in the window at my house, and here I was again. How many people have big white bandages on their faces?

He said something to the driver, and the gray-haired man looked at me with eyes that were calm and dead, and Dodgers Hat pointed his finger at me, like it was a gun, and I screamed, "Fuck you!" like a fool, and started reaching for Lou's gun, and then the Land Rover accelerated and climbed out of view around the next curve.

I quickly went down the hill, found a spot for a U-turn,

which only took about eight back-and-forths, and then I climbed back up the hill, passed 2803, and on a distant ridge I saw a car's headlights, probably the Land Rover's, and I went after it but couldn't catch it. The Land Rover was gone.

3.

AT THE 76 STATION on Beachwood and Franklin, I used a pay phone—a relic from the past—and called the number on the burner phone that had sent the text. I didn't want to use my cell phone back at the house and leave any record of a call. I planned to tell the cops everything, but I also had the instinct, at the same time, to cover my tracks. After two rings, a deep, cautious voice said: "Who is this?"

"I think you can figure it out," I said.

Silence. But he was still there.

"Let's meet. Talk things over," I said. "I like your Dodgers hat. I'm a big Kershaw fan, despite his problems." I was full of bravado and stupidity, and there was more silence. Then I asked: "Why'd you kill my friend?"

That got something out of him. "You're already dead," he said.

I started to blurt out, "Don't you fucking come near my house—"

But he hung up on me, and I didn't think that number would be active much longer. Probably also a burner phone. I tried calling again, but he didn't pick up.

I went back to the house, and George hadn't disturbed Lou's

body, but he knew that something bad had happened: he was subdued and looked at me anxiously. I went into the kitchen and unplugged my phone and called 911. A woman operator answered and I told her that my friend Lou Shelton, an ex-cop, had come to my front door, bleeding from a bullet wound, and had died, and she asked me if the shooter was on the premises and I said no.

Then she asked me if *I* was the shooter and I said no, and when I gave her my name and address, as it was on my driver's license, she wanted to know if "Happy Doll" was a prank, and I said it wasn't a prank, and to please send the cops, my friend was dead in the other room, and then she asked me to stay on the line, but then I lost the connection—fucking cell phones—and I didn't call back.

Then the phone rang—it was 911 trying *me* back—but now that I had made my call, which I should have done immediately, over an hour ago, I was suddenly very nervous and paranoid about everything, and I didn't answer and turned the ringer off. I needed to think and started to pace up and down. My face and my arm were throbbing, trying to knit back together, but it didn't seem wise to take another Dilaudid.

George, sitting still, was watching my every move, like the Mona Lisa, and then he began to trot along with me, and I was really starting to think that it wasn't such a good idea to let the cops know I had gone to 2803 Belden, where I had killed a man.

If I hadn't killed anybody, I could have maybe gotten away with everything I pulled—my friend had just died; I wasn't in my right mind—but throwing that second blonde off the balcony changed everything. I shot Carl Lusk late Tuesday night, and it was now early Friday morning. Could I possibly get away with two self-defense killings in forty-eight hours? I didn't think so.

Plus, I had messed with two crime scenes—my house and Belden—touching everything. More or less framing myself. Who was to say I hadn't shot blondie with Lou's gun? Who was to say I hadn't shot Lou? I could have gotten rid of the .22. The cops would say I was on a spree. Lou and the two blondes. Lusk had just been an appetizer. I could be charged with four murders.

I decided to hide all the evidence.

In my kitchen, hidden in the wall, like a Murphy bed, is an old-fashioned ironing board, which I've never used. The house hasn't changed much since the Rubensteins moved in back in 1950, and for that matter it probably hasn't changed all that much since it was first built in 1923.

So I dumped everything in a plastic bag, except what had been in Lou's pockets, and then hid the bag in the compartment with the ironing board, which has a smell from another time, camphor, maybe, and closed the hidden panel back up.

For no logical reason, I thought the diamond should be hidden somewhere else—like it shouldn't mix with the riffraff of the other items, which meant my logic was stoned logic; everything I was doing was smart if you were stupid—and so I hid the square blue piece of paper in the freezer, in the ice cube receptacle, and didn't think of the irony of hiding a diamond under ice until after I had done it.

Then I put Lou's gun, keys, notebook, and all his other crap back in his pockets and stood there. Like a dumbass. I was trying to think if I knew my story, but I wasn't feeling good at this. I was too high and didn't know what to cover up and what not to cover up. I couldn't think like a cop *or* a criminal, but then I realized that Lou's notebook had the Belden address and that wasn't good, and so I got the notebook out of Lou's pockets, got the bag out from the ironing board, put the notebook in the bag, and put the whole thing back into the secret compartment.

Then I calmed down for a second, like maybe I had covered everything, and I took off my jacket and shoes. This way I'd be in the same state of dress I had been in when Lou first came to the door.

But then I started thinking I didn't want them testing Lou's gun and wondering where he had fired it, all of which could lead them back to the house where I had killed a man.

So I took the Glock out of Lou's pocket and put *that* in the ironing board.

I was now all set to welcome my guests, which was good because George had just started barking. The cops were here.

4.

I HANDLED THE first six uniforms pretty good. They came boiling up the stairs, with their guns out, and George, whom I had quickly stashed in my bedroom, was barking his head off.

I met the cops at the front door and they yelled at me to lie down on the floor.

They frisked me and asked me if I was armed and I said I was not. They asked me if I shot Lou and I said I did not. They asked me this three times and I gave the same answer every time. They asked for my ID, and I directed them to my wallet, which was in my jacket and held two crucial IDs: one that identified me as a licensed private investigator and the other as an ex-cop.

They looked at these things and then let me sit up and get in a chair.

Two of the uniforms took over: a Latina woman, midthirties, named Maria Cole, and her Black male partner, Bill Randle, also midthirties. Cole was small and quiet but looked tough. The strong and silent type. She was also very beautiful, with eerie blue eyes, and just from her bearing she seemed destined to make detective sooner rather than later. Randle was also detective material and movie-star handsome: flawless dark skin, chiseled features. The two of them would have made a beautiful couple, but I sensed no chemistry, no warmth between them.

Randle asked me a two-part question: Did I know who shot Lou and was that individual nearby? I said I didn't know who the shooter was or where it happened; I said Lou showed up at my door, bleeding, out of it, and then he died.

Then they had me tell it from the beginning.

Which I did. And I kept my story real simple:

Lou showed up a little after two a.m., didn't say anything comprehensible, and died on the couch. I went to call 911 but my phone was dead. I returned to the body and lost track of time. I was stunned and in shock. Then my phone was charged and I called.

That's all I told them. I didn't want to fudge the time of death—coroners can be very precise.

By now the house was filled with even more cops and firemen and paramedics, and wrapping up my story, I stood up and said to the two cops, "I really need to take my pain pill: it's been more than six hours, and the face has a lot of nerves," and I pointed to my bandage and headed for the kitchen before they could say anything.

Cole and Randle followed me into the kitchen, and I swallowed a pill dry. I held up the bottle for them to see: "Dilaudid," I said. "They say it's like heroin."

Cole glanced at her partner and then said: "You shouldn't have done that."

"Sorry," I said. But I didn't mean it. I had done it on purpose. For when the detectives showed up, I wanted to plant the seed with these two that I was confused and in pain, and I wanted them to report that to their superiors.

Then if the detectives, who were going to grill me a lot harder than Cole and Randle had, perceived something off in me, I wanted them to think that maybe it was the pills and shock and not the fact that my story was full of holes and lies. It was more of my crazy logic: get fucked up to cover up.

And I looked at Lou in the other room, dead on the couch. If I had just said yes when he came to my office, maybe none of this would have happened. Had he been selling the diamond to raise money to buy a kidney from someone else? And where did he get the diamond?

"If you don't need anything more right now, I'll be upstairs," I said to the two cops. "I got to lie down a second."

Randle said: "The detectives will be here in less than ten minutes. They're going to want to hear everything again."

"I know," I said, and I went upstairs and lay on my bed, and George lay next to me and deposited on my chest, as an offering, a toy, a furry, saliva-drenched skunk, and I said, "Thank you, Georgie-boy," and I dropped it off the side of the bed in such a way that he wouldn't notice, and he put his head on my chest with a sigh, and I felt like he wanted to say: "You shouldn't have lied to the police. You're acting crazy. You're high on Dilaudid and the marijuana you ate."

So then I started thinking that George was right: I *was* acting crazy and this had gone far enough. When the detectives arrived I had better come totally clean: the diamond, Dodgers Hat, 2803 Belden, and the two dead blondes.

That's what I'm gonna do, I thought. *It's the right thing to do. Tell them everything.*

Then I fell asleep, just passed out completely, and when I

woke up, Thode and Mullen were standing above me. Thode still had purple lips and Mullen was still fat. They were the homicide detectives assigned to this murder—Hollywood is a small town, after all—and Thode was leering at me.

So I stuck to my story.

The one filled with lies.

5.

THEY DIDN'T LIKE IT and they still didn't like me.

"He shows up here, says nothing, and just dies?" said Thode, and he blinked twice. Twitchy.

"That's right," I said.

We were still in my bedroom. I was sitting up now, my feet on the floor, and Mullen had sat his big, wide self on the corner of my bed. Thode was in the doorway, two feet away.

I didn't like Mullen touching my comforter with his pants, being anywhere near my bed, and to make things worse George was in his lap, showing no discretion.

"Can we go downstairs?" I said. I wanted to get George off of him.

"Too noisy," said Mullen. "Let's keep chatting here. You got a nice dog. His ears are like velvet. I had a dog but he died."

"Don't say that. George, come here," I demanded. But he just looked at me. He liked the big man. Mullen was probably giving off a lot of good yeasty odors.

Thode said: "So Shelton makes all that effort, climbs your fucking stairs with a bullet having perforated his gut, and then tells you nothing?"

"That's right. Nothing."

"Why does he come to you?"

"I don't know. We were close. He was a cop, you know."

"Good. You were close," said Mullen, and his thick fingers were in George's fur, making love to him. "So any idea who might want Shelton—might want your *friend*—dead?"

"No idea," I said. "George, come here."

"Leave the dog alone," said Mullen. "He's content."

Thode said: "Okay, let's review. Shelton gets here a little after two. Your phone has died and you plug it in and try to stop his bleeding."

"That's right."

"And he says nothing, but then dies, like, two minutes later."

"Right."

"And you don't call for almost an hour."

"I was just sitting with him. He was my friend for twenty-five years. I don't know...I lost track of time. I'm on these pills. I'm a little screwed up. I'm not right."

Mullen looked at me and smiled. "That's the first honest thing you've said."

I didn't have a response to that, and then Thode started in on me again: "You can't think of anybody who would want to take Shelton out? Somebody he owes money to? Somebody with an old beef?"

"I'm telling you, he didn't have enemies."

"So why does he come to you? Why doesn't he drive to a hospital? Are you his best friend?"

"I'm a good friend. But it's not like we were writing love letters every week."

"What kind of guy was he?" asked Mullen.

"Stand-up. Loyal. Smoked too much."

"How'd he keep himself occupied?" Thode asked. "He was retired, and his address is a motel." He produced Lou's driver's license, looked at it: "Mirage Suites, in North Hollywood. What's that about?"

"He worked the desk there at night. He liked working a desk. It's what he did at the Seventy-Seventh. It's how we met."

"Jeez, a real success story like you. A motel clerk."

"Show some respect," I said.

Then Thode, twitch-blinking, looked at his phone, read something. Then he said:

"They sent his file over from the station. Does look like he was a good cop. Put in thirty years. Two citations for bravery. A Medal of Valor in '94 for taking a bullet during a riot"—that would be the bullet he took for me, but I didn't say anything—"and a Police Star in '75, for breaking up a diamond heist downtown and saving his partner, who got shot. Not bad."

Lou had never mentioned anything about this diamond heist and I got a chill down my spine and thought about the bloodstained blue square in my freezer. Then my face must have given something away because Mullen jumped on me:

"What are you thinking? You look scared all of a sudden."

"Not thinking anything except my friend is dead."

But I was thinking that Lou had grabbed a diamond back in 1975 and had been sitting on it for forty-four years. Then, trying to sell the diamond, he'd met with the wrong people. At least four wrong people. The two blondes. And the two in the car: Dodgers Hat and the one with the gray hair.

"Fucking work with us," said Mullen. "You know the guy. He must have been into something. Drugs? Whores? Gambling?"

"Nothing. He had one vice: cigarettes."

6.

AND IT WENT ON like that for a while, the two of them asking me the same questions in different ways, and then they cuffed me—just to be tough—and drove me to Hollywood station. They said the commander wanted to talk to me. In the car, from the front seat, Mullen half joked: "You been keeping us busy this week. A one-man shit show. Got any other homicides you want to tell us about?"

He didn't know how close to the truth he was, and I said: "I got a lead on the Lindbergh baby."

"Who's that?" said Thode.

"Never mind," I said, and we lapsed into silence. I knew they didn't think I had killed Lou or anything like that, but Mullen, especially, could tell I was holding out. He was a good reader of people. His eyes in his big round head were shrewd, and he was one of those types who understood others but not himself. And I'm the same way. I'm not fat, but I have other blind spots.

When we got to the station, they put me in a small, window-less interrogation room and told me to wait. The room was bare and bleak and only had two chairs, one of which I was sitting on. There wasn't even a table.

But so far, so good, I thought. They were just bullying me and had nothing.

Though if they were to interview my neighbors in the morning, I might be in trouble. Somebody could have peeked out and seen me leave and then come back in the Maverick.

But there had been no lights on in any of my neighbors' houses, and cars, at all hours, wander up Glen Alder hoping to find a parking spot but almost never do, and then they make a U-turn in the cul-de-sac. So sounds of cars coming and going wouldn't be paid much attention to, wouldn't be remembered.

Of course, one of my neighbors could have had insomnia and been staring out the window, but...well, I was on the Dilaudid and feeling tough and sort of dreamy. Even the hand-cuffs weren't bothering me.

Then a big man came into the room. One of the biggest I've ever seen, and he closed the door behind him. He was at least six nine, well over 300 pounds, and all of it was hardened with age like a thick tree.

He was in his early sixties—his hair was a grizzled white and cut to the nub like a Marine's. He looked familiar somehow, but I couldn't place him. Which troubled me. You couldn't forget a specimen like this. His chin was huge and jutting, and his large, porous nose, veined by booze, looked like something that sucks along the bottom of an aquarium. His shirtsleeves were rolled up and his old but powerful arms were covered in coarse red hair, like wire.

Where do I know him?

He sidled over to me and stood in front of me. His eyes were close-set and dilated. All iris, no pupil. Black circles.

"You're Hank Doll?" he said. He had a deep voice. Was used to being listened to, obeyed.

"Yeah," I said. "You work with the station commander?"

His answer was a large gun that suddenly blossomed in his hand.

A .357 Magnum with a hard wooden handle.

It had been tucked into the back of his pants, and he shifted the weapon in his hand and took hold of the barrel.

"You're a fucking bastard," he said.

Then he raised the gun into the air above my head, and there was enough time for me to think, *Oh, shit.*

Then he swung the handle down at my face, rotating his hips and putting all his weight into it, like he was swinging a baseball bat, and he aimed the gun handle right for the center of my bandage, and it exploded my wound, and I went flying off the chair and onto the floor.

I was seeing colors and lightning flashes, and I wiggled and crawled like a bug, and then I looked up and he was looming over me, a cruel god, and now I knew why he was familiar. In the father you could see the son. It was Bill Lusk. Carl Lusk's dad.

"I'm sorry about your son," I started to say, but that only seemed to make him more angry. He was wearing heavy black shoes and he kicked me in the head, and I saw what looked like a Ferris wheel made of blood.

Then I went to sleep, but did not dream.

7.

THODE AND MULLEN actually seemed to feel a little bad for me.

They had set me up with Lusk—the commander had no interest in seeing me; that had been a bullshit story—but they didn't know Lusk would fuck me up as much as he did. So they drove me themselves to the Presbyterian and escorted me into the emergency room, flashed their badges, and got me seen right away.

I had told them in the car, "Don't worry—I'm not going to say or do anything," and they seemed to believe me, and they were right to. I'd been a cop once. I wasn't going to sue the LAPD. I couldn't. No matter what. It was a pride thing.

And I didn't take it personally what Lusk had done. He was sick and had raised a son that was sick. His anger was with himself, but he took it out on me. Whatever he had done to his kid years ago, making him weak in the face of adversity, had loaded my gun with that bullet. A bullet that had been looking for him.

But still, I was the one who pulled the trigger. That was *my* sin.

So. Fine. Hit me with your gun. Kick me in the head. I'll take it. There's also a blonde I threw off a balcony that I need to be punished for.

Thode and Mullen left me on my hospital bed—this was getting to be like déjà vu—and Mullen said, in parting: "We still gotta talk about Shelton. You're acting cagey and I don't know why. So don't think we're done with this."

"Okay, sounds good," I said. "I love talking with you two." I was playing the tough guy again, and then the nurses got them out of there.

I only had a mild concussion, which was lucky, and they stitched my face back up and put a fresh bandage on me; they also redressed my arm.

At 6:45 a.m., I left the hospital, even though I wasn't supposed to.

I signed an "against medical advice" waiver, called a Yellow Cab from a pay phone, and went to the spa. I retrieved my car and stopped at the 101 Coffee Shop for scrambled eggs and four cups of coffee. Then I went home: everything was still in the hidden compartment and the freezer.

Lou's blood was on the couch, but he was gone. I didn't feel him in the house anymore.

I fed George and took him for a quick walk.

Then I gave myself a sponge bath, so as not to wet my bandages, got dressed, and headed back out. With George. I didn't want to leave him alone in the house. Dodgers Hat knew where I lived.

I had Lou's gun and diamond and everything else I had grabbed last night.

I got in my Caprice and glanced in the rearview mirror at my face with its new bandage. I put on dark glasses and looked like the invisible man.

But at least you couldn't see the goose egg hidden in my scalp from where Lusk Sr. had kicked me. My hair covered it up and it felt pulpy, like a piece of bad fruit, and my whole head pounded and I dry-swallowed a Dilaudid. I had a lot of ground to cover and wasn't going to let a concussion slow me down.

But what did I think I was going to do? Make things right? Lou was already dead. The time for making things right had passed. There was really only one thing to do now: get to them before they got to me.

8.

I HAD TWO THINGS to work with: the house on Belden and the diamond.

I started with the house.

It was clear and cool out, and I parked the car where I had left it the night before and walked back toward 2803 with George, which was nice cover: a man walking his dog.

In the sunlight, my shoes on the pavement sounded less ominous, and the butterflies were out again, flying drunkenly, impossibly. They filled the air like locusts turned silly.

We went past 2803—there was no police tape or any activity—and we went a little ways down the hill and then doubled back.

The isolation of the house, alone on the edge of the S curve, was more apparent in the daylight. On the side of the road, just before the house, there was an old metal railing. It was meant to keep cars from plummeting over the edge. Since it was a long way down. For a car. Or a body.

We walked past the driveway again and then ducked through the hedges to the front door. The Ken Maurais FOR SALE sign still leaned against the house, but the door was locked. I took out my doohickey, worked the lock, got Lou's gun in my hand, and went inside.

Blondie was gone and there was no blood on the floor. George and I went out to the balcony and looked down. The second blonde was gone, too. Dodgers Hat and the vulture-faced man driving the car—or someone else altogether—had been busy cleaning up. And the cops had been kept out of it.

I looked out over the city. The wind was blowing right, and with all the rain lately you could see clear through to the port of Los Angeles, thirty miles away. You could see the cranes and the tanker ships and the ocean, which was glinting like a strip of silver.

George and I got out of the house and nobody saw us. No cars passed.

Back in the Caprice, I drove over to a side street in Lake Hollywood and parked. It was 8:45. I called a friend, a realtor named Rick Alvarez, who's in his early fifties. A few years ago, Rick's elderly father had bought a bogus coin from a scam artist for fifty thousand cash and the cops didn't do anything about it.

So Dr. Schine sent Rick and his father to me.

It took me a little while, but I found the scam artist in San Diego, my hometown, and I was able to squeeze thirty-eight thousand out of him. The rest had been spent.

Rick was beyond grateful that I had recovered as much as I had, and we've stayed friends since. He's one of those guys who, once you do them a good deed, they're always there for you, and as a licensed realtor he has access to a lot of data-bases, which can be very useful to a private investigator. He's also what I call a good googler. Some people have a knack for it. Not me.

So more than once since I took care of things down in San Diego—though I don't abuse the privilege—I've asked Rick for his help, which he doesn't mind at all. The way he's constructed he acts like he's in debt to me forever, but he also finds the work exciting. Realtors, I've observed, are natural gossips and snoops, and so detective work comes easy to them.

He picked up the phone right away, which is another realtor trait: always available, always working. "Hank," he said. "It's been forever, buddy. I've missed you."

"I know," I said. "It's been a while." Which was true—with my business having slowed down, it had been a long time since I called him.

"Hey, I saw the paper," he said. "You okay?"

"Yeah . . . I wish it hadn't played out the way it did."

"I'm sorry. Anything I can do? You know I'm here for you."

Rick talks fast and moves fast. He's a neat little dark man, built like a bullfighter.

"It's not related to what you saw in the paper, but I need some information on an address: 2803 Belden, in Beachwood Canyon. Can you find out for me who owns it? I think it's for sale or was for sale. Realtor is Ken Maurais."

"Sure, buddy, I got it—2803 Belden. Maurais—sounds familiar. Listen, I gotta meet somebody—a client—in, like, a minute for a coffee, but then I'll get on it and get back to you."

"Perfect," I said. "Talk to you."

We hung up, and George and I got out of the car. It was 8:50, and at nine was my analysis. The side street I had parked on was in front of Dr. Lavich's house. Her office used to be the garage but got renovated forty-plus years ago. She's in her early eighties, been a Freudian analyst a long time.

There's a gate by the side of the office and a little outside waiting area with a bench. I flipped the switch on the wall that lets her know you're out there, and George and I sat on the bench to wait.

He got in my lap, and we were a little early, and I was glad he was with me. Dr. Lavich had heard a lot about George, but, unfortunately, on the day she would finally meet him, I'd also have to say goodbye to her and end my treatment. There was no way my analysis could continue. Not with what I had done in the past twenty-four hours, none of which I could tell her. If I told her, she'd call the police. Immediately.

9.

WHICH IS HOW my therapy had begun four years earlier. I had told her how suicidal I was and some of the plans I had and some of the things I had tried, and she said: "If you keep talking like this, I'm going to call the police right now. It's my obligation. Legally."

"Please, don't do that," I said, suddenly scared, and thought of bolting out of there.

"Then you have to promise me you're not going to kill yourself when you leave here, and you're going to stop talking this way."

That first visit I was sitting across from Dr. Lavich. Later, I'd go to the couch. And you wouldn't have thought it looking at her that day, but she was a tough little lady. She had gold hair and big glasses, and a dog named Janet, a rescue spaniel, was in her lap.

"I promise I won't kill myself," I said. "Please don't call the police. I...I think it was all a cry for help. To myself. I was just going through the motions, without intending to really do it. I was like a child playacting or something. Wanting attention."

What I had done a few days before that had alarmed Dr. Lavich was close my garage door and attach a hose to the exhaust pipe of my car and run it up to the passenger window just to see…what? That it was feasible? Then I had turned on the engine, a sort of test run, and sat in the car for a minute, but scared by what I was doing, I quickly turned the car off.

Then I went inside, put a belt around my neck, and attached it to the pole in my closet and just stood there. Then I undid the belt.

Not liking how either thing had felt—the business in the garage and the business in the closet—I lay on my bed and fantasized about getting my hands on some sedatives and driving out to Malibu, taking the pills, and then swimming out as far as I could, with no hope of making it back, and with the pills making the drowning come easy, like going to sleep. Forever.

All this I had told Dr. Lavich within the first few minutes of meeting her, which had elicited the threat, the very real threat, that she would call the cops, and I was there, ironically, because she was part of an analytic institute that offered free therapy to ex-cops and ex-military.

A social worker at the LAFPP, the pension union for retired cops and firemen, had referred me to Dr. Lavich when I called and said I needed counseling of some sort, and if it hadn't been free, I probably wouldn't have tried analysis and definitely couldn't have afforded it.

But I did give it a try, and the one rule in analysis, Dr. Lavich said early on, was to be totally candid and to hide nothing, which was part of the reason you lie on a couch and don't have to face the analyst. You can just talk and not worry about reading their expression, the look in their eye.

The goal is to free-associate and bring up anything that comes to mind—your daily struggles, neuroses, past events, current events, the smell in the room. Anything.

Freud liked to call it the talking cure, a line he appropriated from one of his early patients, and the idea is that just by talking *every day* to the analyst, who *listens*—it's also a listening cure, in my opinion—you come to know yourself in a way that has eluded you all your life.

And you get truly honest for maybe the first time ever, and through all this talking, you bring the unconscious—all the old injuries and traumas and strange early life misperceptions—to the surface, and you look at everything, the sources of your suffering, like laying out pieces of bone from an archaeological dig.

And by doing this, you slowly lessen the hold the past has on you.

It no longer makes you behave like a puppet, in ways you don't fully understand, and you begin to master compulsions you thought you could never shed.

But what took years—a whole life—to tangle does take a few years to *un*tangle. There's no quick fix, which is why analysis takes time, but you can—if you just talk, hold back nothing, and face what most scares you—shift the course of your life, until you finally untangle, grow up, and wake up.

That's the carrot, at least.

So. The talking cure.

Some of what I had been working on—*talking* about—for four years was this:

My mother's death at my birth.

And how my father hated me—whether he was aware of it or not—for killing her.

They had decided or maybe just joked, while she was pregnant, that they would name the child Happy if it was a boy and Merry if it was a girl. Happy Doll. Merry Doll. Why not Baby Doll? The whole thing was ludicrous, but to honor my mother, my father, Christopher Doll, saddled me with the name Happy but never called me by it. I was either Hapless or Ugly or Merry.

It was always, "Come here, Ugly," and when he especially wanted to humiliate me, he'd say, "Come here, Merry, my sweet girl." So, like something out of Snow White, those were my three names: Hapless, Merry, and Ugly. Though in public he did call me Hank or son.

Both his parents were dead, as were my mother's, so he raised me on his own and often threatened to put me up for adoption, and I wanted him to, but he had some image of himself that wouldn't let him do that. He was a good Catholic *and* he was a Navy man.

Unfortunately, though, for the bulk of his career, because of me, he was stuck behind a desk in San Diego. As a single father, he couldn't ship out anymore, and he never dated or met anyone else. His wife was his Jim Beam, which he came home to every night at 5:30. When I was old enough, starting around age nine, I'd make us dinner at seven sharp and he'd eat a little, drink more, and then pass out on the couch. That was our life together.

Of course, we had some good moments, but when they put my mother in the ground, he went with her. Which was probably the best and noblest thing about him, his love for her, and what was left behind, after my mother died, was more ghost than man.

And so I had begun, in analysis, to forgive him and even to love him.

What else had I worked on with Dr. Lavich?

When I was eleven, a camp counselor orally sodomized me for a month at a Catholic summer camp, which my father had sent me to so as to get me out of his hair.

The next summer, I refused to go to the camp and heard that the counselor—Vince Angelotti was his name—had been arrested, caught with a boy in the shower room. I tried not to think about this for the next few decades, but then a few years ago, when that football coach was arrested in Pennsylvania, I began to feel very anxious and panicky and knew what it was.

So I googled Vince Angelotti, and he came up right away: he was living in Arizona—he was in his late fifties now—and he'd been recently arrested for possession of child pornography and his mug shot was devastating. At camp, he'd been the best athlete and the handsomest of all the counselors, which was great cover for his sickness: all the girls loved him and all the boys worshipped him. He was muscular and olive-skinned, with curly dark hair and pristine features, and then there he was again, on my computer, thirty-odd years later.

But he was barely recognizable. Time had just about destroyed him. Yet he was in there. In that mask. Behind that mask. *I* could see him. *I* hadn't forgotten.

His age was listed as fifty-seven, but he looked much older, and he had grown more feminine over time, witchlike. His dark hair was cut short and his skin was yellow-gray and his cheeks were sunken, eaten away from the inside, and his nose was misshapen, most likely from snorting drugs, and his eyes, the way they peered into the camera, were defiant: he couldn't yet relinquish what he craved, and it looked as if his eyebrows and eyelashes had been boiled off. One could imagine that he had been soaked in formaldehyde while still alive.

Oddly, there was a slight trace of a smile for the mug-shot camera, some old reflex for when your picture is taken and you try to look nice, and I could see in that pitiful smile some lingering wish to be loved and to have never been cursed this way.

But I might have been projecting.

What else?

When I was fourteen, our church assigned me a Big Brother, Kyle Corcoran, who was eighteen. No one had ever been kinder to me. We played catch together and rode bikes, went surfing and skateboarding.

Then after three months of this, of what felt like heaven to me, he hanged himself in his parents' basement, and no one knew why he had done it. Kyle seemed perfect: he was an Eagle Scout and straight-A student and a Big Brother. But then someone started the rumor that he had killed himself because he was gay and didn't want to tell his parents, who were very religious.

After he died, I intermittently thought about suicide— hanging, specifically, just like Kyle—for the next thirty-two years, but talking to Dr. Lavich had finally brought the decades of suicidal ideation to an end.

Then when I was eighteen, to get away from my father, I joined the Navy, only to find myself, three months later, stuck on a ship of men just like him.

A month after that, my father died, unexpectedly. We were docked in Seoul when they informed me, and he and I hadn't exchanged a single letter while I had been away, and I had never called home. I never got to say goodbye, and I hadn't said "I love you" in years. When I got the news, I wished I could have told him that one more time.

So I did seven years in the Navy, which were fairly hellish: I was a loner and all screwed up. Because I wasn't popular with my fellow sailors (I was too bookish, too self-absorbed), the master-at-arms on my ship—the naval equivalent of a military policeman—saw me as a natural fit and recruited me.

I was big and strong, which was mostly what they looked for in a cop on a boat, and they wanted someone who wouldn't play favorites and be close to the men, which was another box I had already checked. They sent me to masters-at-arms school in San Antonio at the end of my first year, and the next six years I spent as a policeman on different ships, mostly serving in the Pacific.

When I got out, I followed a girl from San Diego to Los Angeles, didn't know what to do with myself, and joined the LAPD for the next ten years. The bulk of my career was spent trying to find missing children—maybe because of the whole Vince Angelotti thing—and it got to me. Seemed like I was working in a slaughterhouse every day. My job was to stop the butchers, but it was like a bad dream: get one kid off the meat hook and here come ninety-nine more.

So the suicidal ideation was around-the-clock back then, and I drank heavily and became a pothead, and all I wanted, I thought, was a girlfriend. That would make everything okay, but I could never make a relationship last. It's really not possible when you hate yourself.

At thirty-five, I quit the cops and life got a little better. I liked working for myself, and Dr. Schine sent a lot of business my way. I was a functional alcoholic and pothead, and my love life was busy, though really it was a version of that children's book where that little bird—not knowing what he is—goes around saying to all the other animals something like: "Are you my mommy?"

Then, when I was forty-six, it all came crashing down bad. It was like a story out of myth. I had met the girl of my dreams but didn't know it. I had waited all my life to meet her—maybe ever since my mother's death—and then when she was right in front of me I couldn't see it.

Her name was Joyce and she taught high school English and, like me, she loved books. It was a shared hobby and we would read in bed together, and she was smart and sweet and pretty, and I loved talking to her, and I would bound to the door when she came to my house, excited to see her, and yet for some self-destructive reason, I also kept her at a distance: wouldn't answer all her calls; would only see her once or twice a week. And yet she was still crazy about me. She would tell me she loved me, and I wouldn't or couldn't say it back.

I even had the audacity after we had been together awhile—I was insane—to suggest we have an open relationship. I had never tried it before and was going through some moronic phase, thinking that maybe the cause of all my years of failed romances was monogamy, which was, of course, totally wrong. The problem was me. Always had been.

So with all my pushing her away, Joyce, finally, in part because of my stupid suggestion about being open, took up with another guy, fell for him, and ended *our* relationship.

And then it hit me: I'm in love with her. I never was so sure of anything in my whole life. Of course, I was half-deluded— what did I know of love?—but the pain was real, and I sent her letters and diaries and asked her to come back to me. But it was too late. She was in love with someone else, and, anyway, why should she give me another chance? I hadn't valued her the first time.

And this broke me.

I couldn't forgive myself for losing her, and the pain of my whole strange, desperate life came flying out of me.

Which is when I put the hose in the car exhaust.

Which is when I went into the closet and played at hanging myself, like my old hero, Kyle Corcoran.

And which is when I ended up in Dr. Lavich's office and slowly began a four-year process of rebuilding myself—a reconstruction project that I had just torn down in a single night.

A little after nine, she opened the door to her office and said, brightly, "Hello, Hank," as she always did. Analysts like being alive. At least, Dr. Lavich does. Then she took in the big bandage on my face and the dog in my arms, and she said, with concern, "What's going on?" It was clear that she hadn't seen yesterday's *LA Times*.

"I have some things to tell you," I said, and stood up. She nodded and stepped to the side, and I went into her office.

10.

I LAY ON the couch, and George said hello to Janet by sniffing her anus. In return, she licked his penis, and then he jumped on top of me and lay on my belly like a sphinx, a favorite position of his.

Janet went off to squeeze in next to Dr. Lavich, who sat behind me in her chair, silently, and we made a nice little picture, I imagined, with our dogs, which was fitting because Freud famously loved dogs, always had one in his office and thought they were calming for his patients and a good judge of character. Freud is Dr. Lavich's hero, and there are a few pictures of him—though none with dogs—on the walls of her office, which is quite large and filled with books and odd paintings and sculptures. It's a bright room, because of a skylight in the ceiling, and in the corner are old stuffed animals from when she used to work with children.

The couch I lay on was simply a soft blue leather couch, cracked with age, and across from the head of the couch was a poster, under glass, of a Chagall painting, which I had stared at for four years—it was directly in my line of vision. At the center of the painting, at the center of a somewhat surreal landscape, a man and woman sit on a bench in front of a house. The man has his arm around the woman and she leans into him, with love and trust and perhaps some sadness and fear.

And that day I stared at the painting as I always did. At the man and the woman. And I thought of Monica. And I could hear Dr. Lavich breathing. Sometimes she had the sniffles, which bothered me, neurotically.

I wasn't sure where to begin or what to say.

I've killed two men since I've seen you last. Also, my friend died, more or less in my arms, and he had come to me a few days before and asked me for a kidney and if I had said yes right away, if my first instinct had been generosity, he probably wouldn't have gotten killed, and one of the men I killed was strangling a girl at work and then he nearly killed me, he cut me with a very large knife, and I shot him, though I didn't mean to kill him, I just wanted to slow him down, and then his father beat me, and I have a prescription for Dilaudid, and I know you think I still drink too much and smoke too much, but I really like this Dilaudid, it puts two inches of gauzy curtain between me and the world, and, oh, one good thing is Monica, you know my friend from the bar, the last woman I slept with, four years ago, well, maybe she loves me or maybe, which is more likely, she pities me…but I think I love her, which I didn't think I could feel again…I put my face in her neck, and it felt so good…but I have to get to these men, the ones who killed my friend, before they get to me, but maybe what I'm trying to do is kill myself and I'm utterly deluded…deluded on Dilaudid…maybe that's why they call it Dilaudid, because it makes you deluded…though it hasn't occurred to me, until just now, that I could take these pills to Malibu and swallow all of them, like my old plan, and swim out into the ocean and…but I don't want to do that; I want to hunt these men down, and I didn't tell you but the second man I killed I threw off a balcony and his neck broke at the most hideous angle, and there was another man in the house, with a bullet in his head, fired by the gun in my pocket…I'm sorry I brought a gun into your office…

But I didn't say any of that to her, though that's what was unspooling in my crazy mind.

Finally, she spoke: "Hank, tell me what's going on. Why did you bring your dog, and what happened to your face?"

I touched the bandage. Could feel the raised, long pucker of the stitches beneath the cotton. I said: "I can't tell you anything. You'll have to trust me on this. So I'm going to sit up in a second and leave. My analysis, unfortunately, has to stop."

She waited a moment. Then she said: "You can tell me what's going on."

"I can't. I have to stop seeing you."

"I'm very concerned for you right now, Hank. Please tell me—"

I stood up abruptly with George and walked to the door without looking at her.

"Hank!" she said with urgency, standing.

I couldn't look her in the eye and said, without turning, keeping my back to her: "Please; you have to trust me. Thank you for all you've done for me. I have to go now," and then I said, in a whisper she couldn't hear, "I love you," and then I quickly opened the door and walked rapidly to my car, George trailing after me. What a fool I must have looked like. A scared little man—at six two, 190—running away from a tiny analyst. A Freudian with gold-colored hair.

She followed me as far as her driveway and called out: "Hank, please, let me help you!"

But I didn't turn. I got into the car and drove away without looking back.

11.

IT WAS TWENTY MINUTES north on the 101 to Tarzana and the Vault Pawn Shop, which had a big glittery sign in its window: WE WILL BUY YOUR GOLD.

The owner of the shop, Rafael Mendes, who goes by Rafi, likes to tell people that his last name is spelled with an *s* and not a *z*. It's a real sore spot for him—we all have our areas of frustration—but, regardless, he's a good friend of mine and always behind the counter.

I met him in 2001 when his niece, Dolores, ran away, and he came to Hollywood looking for her—a family friend had spotted her on a bus. My partner and I were assigned the case—I was still a cop then—and we found her working in a strip club off Hollywood Boulevard. She was fifteen years old.

Rafi and his sister, the girl's mother, collected her at the station, and Rafi and I had stayed in touch all these years, initially bonding over an old Rolex I was wearing back then. I had won the watch at a poker game with a bunch of other cops during my Texas Hold'em phase, and Rafi had given me his card and told me if I ever wanted to sell it to come see him. He collects and repairs Rolexes, as a hobby and a business, and holds on to them, selling one off every once in a while, like playing the stock market, when the timing—no pun intended—seems right.

So a few months after finding his niece, Dolores, I had started to bottom out on my little gambling phase, racking up some nice debt, and I remembered his card in my wallet. I drove out to Tarzana and sold him the watch for two grand. Ten years later, he sold it for $4K. Which is why he's a Rolex man. They age well.

Anyway, I got a kick out of him from the very first time he came into the station: he's eccentric and pint-size, but the way he carries himself, he seems a lot bigger, and I like eccentrics, people with style, always have, and over the years, I've pawned a few things with him and we've had a few meals together, and every now and then he's assisted me on a case. A pawnbroker, like a real estate agent but in different ways, can be helpful in the detective business. Rafi knows where to get things, and he understands people: their vulnerability, their corruption, *and* if they have any good in them. He takes their confessions—and their possessions—like a pawnshop priest.

His store is in a little strip mall on Reseda Boulevard, and as I parked in the spot right in front of his glass doors, I realized that what I had just executed was more of a swerve than a direct line. The Dilaudid I had taken earlier was circulating freely now, impairing my driving, and my legs felt heavy.

I then cracked the window, got out of the Caprice, and told George to stay.

Rafi had a cat hidden somewhere in the store, and George would sniff him out in a second and tear the place apart.

He looked heartbroken to be left behind, and I said, trying

to be firm, "You'll be all right, George. I won't be too long—I promise." But I wasn't able to maintain eye contact, and I closed the door, locking him in.

As I entered the pawnshop, I dared to look back and George was standing with his paws on the dashboard, staring at me intently.

"I love you! I won't be long," I said loudly, trying to reassure him.

Then I walked into the Vault—it was just a little before 9:30—and it was empty except for Rafi, behind the glass counter.

"Oh, my God, Hank," he said. "What happened to your face? Skin cancer?"

There was a mirror behind the counter—behind Rafi—and I could see that my bandage was turning a little pink with seepage. "It's a long story, but I got cut bad," I said. "You didn't see the paper?"

"I never look at it anymore; too depressing," he said.

Rafi's in his early sixties, gray-haired, cherub-faced, and all of five four, which makes the sapphires and gold rings on his hands look even bigger. His large brown eyes hide behind orange-framed women's glasses, and he's in possession of a perfectly round little belly, which he's always cupping with his bejeweled hands.

He also has beautiful white teeth, which he puts in a cup at night, and he's been with the same man, Manuel, for forty years, but his mother is still alive so they haven't gotten married. Though they do live with her, in her house, and she gives them dinner in front of the television every night.

"So who cut you?" he asked. "It was in the paper?"

"You know I've been working over at that spa, and a client went berserk," I said. "But to be honest, it's too much to go into, and there's something I really need you to look at."

"Have you been drinking? You sound funny."

"Sorry—it's the pill for my face," I said. "It's as strong as heroin, but you take it like Motrin." Then, with thick fingers, I took the folded blue piece of paper out of my pocket—the bloodstains had turned brown—and he said: "What's on the paper? Mud?"

"Yeah," I said, and showed him the diamond. His eyes widened, and I said, "What do you think of it?"

"If it's real—and it looks real—it's worth a lot of money," he said in awe. "Let's go to my office."

He locked his front door, and we went to the back, past the long glass cases of jewelry and watches—that's primarily what Rafi trades in—and we settled ourselves in his cluttered little work space, him behind the desk, me in front of it. An old oil painting of Jesus, dim with age, was on the wall behind Rafi, watching over us.

He took some tweezers and put the diamond in a small metal cup on a scale. He peered closely at the instrument and said: "This is a very big and beautiful girl. Seven carats. And if she weighs this much, she's real."

"How much would that go for?"

"On weight alone we're talking fifty, sixty thousand dollars," he said, which was the amount that Lou had been tossing around when he came to see me. "But this diamond has other qualities. Let's take a closer look."

Rafi then swiveled in his chair. To his left, on a wing of his desk, was a large microscope. He put the diamond where it needed to go and bent over the lens and fiddled with the thing. He was still a moment. Then he said: "Magnificent. Come see."

I came around the desk, feeling a little wobbly, like a drunk, and I peered through the microscope at the diamond, and it was like looking into the Hall of Mirrors in Versailles.

"So beautiful," I said, and it was moving to look at, this glimpse of nature from deep in the earth. I had never seen a diamond under a microscope before, and then I noticed that at the edge of the Hall of Mirrors there seemed to be lettering of some kind. "What's that marking on the side?"

We switched places, and Rafi, his eye still on the microscope, said: "I didn't see it before, but you're right. It's been lasered. On what you call the girdle. Lasered by GIA." He said each letter like you'd say CIA. "That's the highest standard there is. This diamond's been certified."

I went back to my chair, and Rafi, with great respect, returned the diamond to the middle of the blue piece of paper, which lay on the center of his desk between us. I said: "I also have this," and I took out the brochure with the letters GIA on the front.

"Yeah, that's the cert," he said, looking at the brochure. "GIA grades diamonds, jewels, everything, and what they say goes, and the laser marks it, like a cattle brand. They just started doing that a few years ago."

"It doesn't lessen the value?"

"No. It increases it."

"And this place is down in Carlsbad?" He said it was, and I asked him: "Does GIA stand for something?"

"Gemological Institute of America," he said. "They're like the Fort Knox of jewels. Where did you get this diamond? The cert says Louis Shelton."

"That's my friend. He died last night and gave it to me."

Rafi looked at me. "Gave it to you?"

"He asked me to sell it for his daughter. Kind of a deathbed request. So does that report say how much it's worth? I didn't see a price."

"GIA doesn't estimate prices. They just grade the diamond, based on industry standards, and then the market determines the price. What I can do is put what's in this report"—he lifted the brochure—"into a website, Blue Nile Diamonds. I've used it before but never for anything this big, and they give you a price, based on other diamonds in the market with similar ratings. It's like a search engine."

He studied the report for a moment and then said: "See? It has a D rating for color, which is the highest, means it's *without* color, and it's VVS1, which means it's nearly flawless, no little puckers or marks of any kind. I think we're looking at a lot of money here."

Excited, he took a laptop out of his desk drawer, did some typing, and his rings made little metallic noises that were pleasing. Then he pivoted the computer so I could see the Blue Nile web page. "See? It says its diamonds are all GIA graded."

Then he swung the laptop back around and did some more typing, stared a moment at the computer, while it must have been searching, and then he slid back in his chair. "Jesus, Hank," he said. "A comparable diamond, emerald cut, that weight, has sold for $289,000. Now, that's retail. So wholesale, what you could get is more like two hundred, probably. This is way above anything I do."

We both stared at the little chip of ice on his desk, at $289,000 worth of sparkling carbon. Which up close, under a microscope, looked like a palace.

Then I said: "Where would I sell it? A fence?" I was thinking that the team operating out of the house on Belden was some kind of high-end fence.

Rafi looked at me like I was crazy. "A fence? No! You've got a cert! You're legit. You want to sell it, you should go to the diamond district, a diamond dealer, or I guess you could go to an auction house, like Christie's, but they would take a cut. Probably 20 percent. Best bet is a diamond dealer. No cut."

"So my friend wouldn't have gone to a fence if he was looking to raise some cash?"

"No—no reason to go to a fence," Rafi said, and he lowered his orange glasses and looked at me with something behind his eyes. "This cert is like a passport or a birth certificate. He could just go downtown to the diamond district."

When he said "downtown," an idea sparked in my dull head. I took Lou's notebook out of my pocket and said: "Can you google something for me?"

He said he would, and I read him the first address Lou had scrawled: 550 Hill Street, suite 834. Rafi's fingers made their noise on the keypad and then he said: "Yes, that's a diamond dealer. Raz Diamonds. Probably Israeli. And that address is at the center of the district."

I nodded and folded the diamond into the blue paper and sat there a moment, thinking. I was deep in the Dilaudid and everything going on. *Lou. The two dead blonde men. A stolen diamond.* Then Rafi said: "Are you all right, Hank? You seem...I don't know."

"I apologize, Raf. It's the pill; it's got me feeling a little loopy," I said.

"I'm worried about you, Hank. Who takes care of you?"

"What do you mean? Nobody takes care of me. I have my dog."

"A dog is good, but a person is better. I wish you had a person."

I stood up, pocketed the diamond and the cert, and said: "Don't worry about me, Rafi. You know I'm always all right."

"But what have you gotten into this time? How did your friend die?"

"I'll tell you later, okay?"

He knew I was protecting him—better he not know too much—and he shook his head, concerned but also stoic. He's survived a long time in that pawnshop and always has a nice little Beretta strapped to his ankle.

He pushed himself up from his desk and walked me out, and as he unlocked the door, he said: "You need to get that somewhere safe. Diamonds get people hurt."

Then he noticed the butterflies in the parking lot, swirling about like drunken particles, and he gestured toward them and said: "Must be the end of the world."

"Must be," I said, and we shook hands goodbye.

12.

I GOT IN the Caprice and George gave me lots of kisses, grateful for my return, and Rafi was still standing behind his glass doors, looking at me. Our eyes met and then he disappeared into the shadows of his pawnshop, and then my phone started ringing. It was Rick Alvarez.

"Got anything?" I said by way of answering.

"Not anything too good," he said. "The Belden house is owned by a private anonymous trust. I was able to find out that the trust is repped by a Beverly Hills law firm: Stamm, Baker, Landis, and at least eight other names. I'm not kidding. So I called the firm and the receptionist sent me to the voice mail of one of their lawyers. Thing is, if he does get back to me, I doubt he'll tell me anything. And because it's private, there are really no public records I can access. Wish I had more for you."

"It's all right; I appreciate it," I said. "I'll go up against that Ken Maurais, see what he can tell me."

"Okay. Next couple of hours, I gotta show some houses to this client over in Echo Park and then Highland Park, but then I'll do some more digging for you. Some other angles. See if

I can find anything. It's unlikely, but I'll try. And just so you know, tomorrow I'm going down with my wife to Costa Rica. But maybe I can find something today."

I thanked him and we hung up, and then on my phone I searched "Ken Maurais" and got his office number and address, which was on Hillhurst over in Los Feliz. My battery was running low again—I was already at 10 percent—but I didn't have time to go to a Sprint store and get the thing fixed. I called the Maurais number—putting in *67 first to set my phone to "private"—and a young-sounding woman answered: "Ken Maurais."

"May I speak to Mr. Maurais?"

"He's not in right now, but can I take a message?"

"I was hoping to meet with Mr. Maurais. A friend recommended your agency, said Ken did a great job, and I'm looking for a house in the two to three to four million range, something with a pool." I wanted to sound like an enticing potential client.

"We can help you with that, definitely. Mr. Maurais can call you. What's your number—"

"What if I just swing by today? What time will he be in?"

"He can call you first if you like—"

"I'll just come by. What time will he be in?"

"Well...he should be back around twelve, and he's here all afternoon—"

"Great. I'll come by at noon."

"Are you sure he can't call you first—"

"I'm sure," I said firmly.

There was silence. Then, worn down, she said: "Your name, sir?"

I looked at George. "George," I said, and George perked up

his ears. "George Mendes. With an *s*, not a *z*. But you know what? My phone is dying, so I better go. Thank you so much; see you at twelve," I said, and hung up.

It was now 9:50, and I got back on the 101 and pointed the Caprice south to downtown, to Hill Street and Raz Diamonds.

13.

TRAFFIC WAS LIGHT, but I wasn't happy with the way I was driving.

The accelerator felt like it was made of thick rubber and I had no feel for it. The Dilaudid had me hidden inside myself, far away from my extremities, and the coffee I had drunk earlier had died on me completely.

It was like I was pushing all four thousand pounds of the Caprice myself. Everyone was passing me, and I wanted to go faster but I was also scared to.

Nervous, I stayed in the right-hand lane and tried not to kill anyone.

Then I remembered I had a few Adderall in the glove compartment. A friend had given them to me during the previous tax season when I couldn't stop procrastinating, but I had never taken any.

Normally, I don't like speed, but I thought the Adderall and the Dilaudid might balance each other out. The Dilaudid would be for the pain and the Adderall would keep me going, which is all to say that when Carl Lusk had cut me, he must have nicked some of my brain, because I was on a record streak of stupidity.

One hand on the wheel, I reached across George and in doing so nearly drove into the embankment, but then I righted the car, while horns blared, and I fished the bottle out of the glove compartment, wading through a ton of crap I had shoved in there.

The bottle said to take one pill, but that's if you're *not* on Dilaudid, and so I took *two,* and George looked at me and said, "What are you doing? I've never seen you like this," and then Dr. Lavich called, which was perfect timing.

I felt caught like a child and, of course, I didn't pick up, but I listened to her voice mail. She sounded upset, in a way I had never heard before: all her training had made her unflappable, but I had rattled her with my dramatics, and in her voice mail she insisted that I check in with her and let her know that I was all right.

I hated upsetting her, but I wasn't going to call her back. I was officially off the rails, which was the only way I could keep doing what I was doing, which, on a conscious level, was to retrace Lou's movements until they led me to Dodgers Hat and the gray-haired man and which, on an *unconscious* level, was to make a very bad situation far worse.

But the act of taking the double dose of Adderall, before it could even kick in, did seem to wake me up in a placebo sort of way, and we made it downtown, thankfully, without killing anyone, in twenty-five minutes. The LA freeway system, when it works, is a marvel, on the order of the Great Wall of China.

At 3rd Street, we exited the 101, and I found an open meter about a block from 550 Hill, which was a large modern glass building across from Pershing Square.

We got out of the car and started walking and George

urinated several times where other dogs, like Masons, had left secret messages, and then we got to 550 and sailed across the lobby, where a large sign informed me that this building was the International Jewelry Center.

There was security behind a counter, but you didn't have to check in; you could go straight to the elevator bank, and no one made a fuss about George, perhaps because he was so elegant looking, though, of course, dogs are everywhere these days. People are so insane and confused that they need them more than ever.

In the crowded elevator, I noticed that the man in front of me had in his hand a thick roll of money, the width of a soup can. He got off at the sixth floor, and George and I got off at the eighth.

The hallway was long and nondescript and wrapped around the building in a gigantic rectangle, which I discovered since we took the long way to suite 834, passing many office doors, including one with a plaque that said: DIAMOND CENTER SYNAGOGUE.

I stopped for a moment in front of the synagogue and touched the mezuzah on the doorframe in honor of my dead Jewish mother, with the selfish intention that maybe she or God might look after me.

Finally, we found 834. The door had no signage, but there was a button to push and another mezuzah. I pushed the button, and the lock clicked.

I opened the door and on my way in I touched this second mezuzah for another dose of good luck and blessing, and then put my fingers to my mouth and kissed them in case I was on camera, which I imagined I was.

A friend told me once that you first touch the mezuzah

to remind you of God, and then you kiss your fingers to show your love for God, and I thought it might be good, if anyone was watching, to exhibit familiarity with this custom, and on the other side of the door George and I found ourselves in a small vestibule with a bulletproof glass window, and next to that was a connecting door to the interior of the office.

I stood in front of the window, which had a thin opening at the bottom for passing thin items. An accented voice spoke to me out of a speaker, which I couldn't locate, and the voice said: "What do you want? Do you have an appointment?"

I fished the diamond out of my pocket, found a camera lens in the corner of the vestibule, and held up the glinting piece of carbon to the camera's glass eye. I became aware that I was starting to grind my teeth and swivel my jaw from the Adderall, and I said: "I'm looking to sell this diamond."

There was no response from the Wizard of Oz, and then a man, early thirties, dark-haired and trim, appeared on the other side of the glass and said, with an Israeli accent: "We don't see people without appointments."

"Lou Shelton told me to come here," I offered by way of explanation, and then took a risk and said, even though I couldn't be sure it was true: "He came here yesterday, with this," and I held up the big diamond again, like $289,000 worth of bait.

The diamond intrigued him for sure, and he looked me over, taking in the stained bandage on my face and the attractive dog on the leash.

And while he looked at me, I looked at him.

He was wearing an expensive tailored white shirt, and he wasn't tall, but he was built like a knife. I figured that not too long ago he would have been a soldier in the IDF, and he still looked like a soldier: his hair was cut close to his head; his dark features were handsome and severe.

After a few seconds of our staring contest, he nodded, which was his way of saying he trusted me enough to let me in, and his hand reached down below my line of sight, and he must have pushed a button, because the lock on the connecting door clicked loudly.

George and I went through the door, and the dark-haired man was already walking down the hallway ahead of us and said over his shoulder: "Come into my office." To go with his crisp white shirt, he wore tailored blue pants and Italian loafers the color of raw steak. He moved catlike and easy.

We passed two closed doors, and then at the end of the corridor was his office, which had a view overlooking Pershing Square and all of downtown, but that was it for frills. The carpet was old and thin, and the walls were bare and scuffed and needed painting. One got the sense that the goal here was to make money, not spend it.

The only thing in the room was a large black desk, with an office chair on each side, and even the desk was mostly barren. The only things on it were a lamp, a scale, and in the corner of the desk—angled so that I could just about see the whole thing—was a very small CCTV monitor, which was split into four live feeds: the vestibule, the interior hallway, and two offices, which were probably behind the doors we passed.

In the two offices, men sat at desks, looking at computer monitors. The dark man in front of me could watch his colleagues, and they could probably watch him, and if he had been looking he had probably seen me kiss my fingers when I entered the vestibule.

He sat down and I sat down and he looked me over again. He liked to do a lot of looking. It was a power move, and it came to him naturally. Then he said: "What's your name?" He spoke with a kind of hoarseness in his voice.

"Hank Doll," I said.

"Doll?"

"Yeah. It's Irish. But my mother was Jewish."

He said, noncommittal: "That's nice."

"And you're Israeli?" I said. "Ex-military?"

"Yes. We're all ex-military."

"You've got a military bearing."

He shrugged that off and said: "Your name is really Doll?"

"Yes. It really is."

A smile, which he then tried to suppress, cracked his facade. To a foreigner the name Doll can be especially funny, but he had seen the diamond, and while my showing up unannounced had made him wary, he also didn't want to offend me. It was a very big diamond.

So he covered the smile by reaching his hand across the desk and saying: "I'm Yair. Yair Raz."

"The Raz of Raz Diamonds?"

"No. That's my father. But he lives in Antwerp. I run the Los Angeles office."

We shook—he had a strong grip—and then he leaned back in his chair and did some more appraising. When he tired himself out with that, he said: "What happened to your face?"

"Skin cancer," I said.

He nodded as if he understood, and then he said, still wondering if he should trust me: "And why is your mouth moving like that? Are you on drugs?"

"No. Nothing like that. It's Adderall for the pain. My skin cancer."

"For the pain?"

"You're right. I'm taking something else for the pain and the Adderall is so that I'm not sleepy from the pain pill. See what I mean? They work together. On the pain. But it's got me a little speedy."

Then George jumped on my lap, and Yair said: "What's your dog's name?"

"George," I said, and I put him back down on the floor.

"He has beautiful eyes."

"Yeah," I said. "But no flirting. I get jealous." The Adderall was really enjoying itself, had me flapping my mouth, had me feeling blithe and clever.

But Yair didn't understand my joke and so he pretended I hadn't spoken. Then he said, with some condescension: "You take him everywhere? He's a support dog?"

"Yeah, because of my face cancer."

That threw him, and I could see he was thinking I was half nuts, but cancer gives people pause. He shrugged without realizing it, brushing the whole odd conversation to the side. He was ready to get down to business. He said: "Can I see the diamond?"

I handed it to him and he produced a cloth and tweezers from his desk drawer. He wiped the stone with the cloth and took hold of it with the tweezers and held the diamond under the lamp, which I realized was a special lamp, with probably a very specific spectrum of light.

Then a small jeweler's loupe seemed to materialize from nowhere in his other hand and he looked at the stone with the seriousness of an expert. "I saw this diamond yesterday," he said, still admiring it under the loupe, and then he deposited the diamond in the metal cup on the scale and said: "Yeah. Seven carats. Same diamond."

He left it in the cup and didn't hand it back to me. Another power move. "So why are you here?" he asked.

"Lou Shelton died last night. In the hospital. A brain aneurysm. He was awake for a little while and gave me the diamond and asked me to sell it. For his daughter. An hour later, he died."

"He was your friend?"

"My best friend."

"I'm sorry," he said, and there was a trace of feeling behind it. Then he said: "Strange I should meet him yesterday and now he's dead. He said he found us in the phone book. First time I heard this. I didn't know there were phone books anymore."

That sounded right. Lou was from another generation. There are late adopters and no adopters and that's what Lou was, a no adopter. He always kept a phone book in his room at the motel, and I could see him looking up "diamonds" in the Yellow Pages, running his finger down the line and stopping at Raz Diamonds just because he might have liked the sound of the name.

"He was an old-fashioned sort of guy," I said. "We were cops together."

"He told me he was an ex-cop."

"I was a rookie when I met him. He actually saved my life. Took a bullet for me."

I thought all this would appeal to the ex-soldier, make me trustworthy, even though my jaw was swiveling, and he nodded at my sob story, just as he had at my cancer story, and then he said: "It's a very beautiful diamond. Mr. Shelton said it was his grandmother's, in the family a long time, and I offered to buy it yesterday, but he said he wanted to shop it around."

"I don't know about that. He told me to come to you."

"You have the cert?"

I took it out and handed it to him. He looked at it. The cert seemed to complete his transformation from wary to trusting. It was as Rafi said: the cert was a passport, a golden ticket. He said: "So you want to sell it?"

"Lou didn't tell me how much you offered. Just told me to come to you. He was pretty weak and kept going in and out of consciousness."

"Two hundred thousand dollars is what I offered. It's what anyone in this building would offer. I told him that. In the diamond business we don't lie. It's the only way to survive."

"Blue Nile says it could go for two eighty-nine."

"You did some research. That's nice. But that's retail. I have to make a living. Go shop around if you want—everyone will tell you two hundred. But I'll offer cash. Most places don't do that, but I know people prefer cash."

"Two twenty?" I said. I was flying by the seat of my pants. I had gotten out of him what I thought I needed—Lou had been here, didn't take his offer, and shopped it elsewhere. On Belden Drive? But why?

Maybe Rafi was wrong and Lou had *wanted* to go to a fence. Maybe he'd come here just to get a price, to get a sense of the marketplace, and then he'd gone to the fence because he'd stolen the diamond forty-five years ago, was still afraid to get caught, and thought a fence was safer than a legit dealer.

I knew for a fact that the grandmother story was a lie: Lou was raised in an old-fashioned orphanage and never even got adopted, maybe because he was a runt.

"I can't do two twenty," he said. "Two hundred cash. You go somewhere else, they will tell you the same. We all know each other. Also, Blue Nile gives the absolute highest price possible, which you almost never get. You can shave twenty thousand off their prices every time. So I'm not trying to steal from you. Also think about it: with cash you can avoid taxes, so two hundred cash is like two sixty, two eighty. It's a very good offer, my friend."

I looked at him and then made a stab in the dark: "Do you live in Beachwood Canyon on Belden Drive? I feel like I've seen you when I walk my dog."

His look of utter bewilderment told me that he had no connection to the house with the two dead blondes, and he said, dismissively: "I live in Calabasas. So are we doing business?" He was a good salesman—or in this case buyer—and he was trying to close.

"Can I think about it a second?"

He stood up quickly, like a knife opening. "Sure. Think about it. You want an espresso? I love espresso. It's the one thing I hate about America. The coffee."

"Yes, thank you," I said. "I'd like an espresso."

He came around the desk, and George stood up and put his paws on Yair's tailored blue slacks and sniffed his zipper for traces of urine.

Yair smiled and petted him and said: "Handsome dog."

"No flirting," I repeated, and Yair's eyes crinkled at me in confusion, and he left the room. I watched the monitor and saw him go into one of the offices. His colleague looked up from his computer, and Yair made his way to a counter, where there was an espresso machine.

Then I looked out the window and a few hapless butterflies went by like something out of a cartoon. The Dilaudid and the Adderall were having a wrestling match inside me to see who was in charge—I felt dull and sharp simultaneously—and there was also the constant sensation, which had started last night after Lou died, of watching myself at some remove, as if I were on CCTV in my own mind.

But I had a decision to make: sell the diamond and bring the money to Lou's daughter, which *was* Lou's actual deathbed request, or hold on to it for the inevitable reckoning with the cops. Or could I avoid a reckoning?

Yair came back into the room with the espressos and I said: "We're in business."

"Excellent," he said, and there was a cocky gleam in his eye. He lived for moments like this: making the deal was confirmation of his abilities.

He put my espresso down in front of me. "You made the right decision," he said, and went to his side of his desk, smiled at me, and raised his espresso cup. I raised mine in salute and we sipped our coffees.

Then he removed from his desk a small box for the diamond and picked it out of the metal cup with the tweezers, but he must have squeezed a little too hard—he was more excited than he wanted to let on—because the diamond flipped into the air and caught a few beams of light and then fell to the carpet. I gasped, and George made a lunge for it, but I yanked on his leash just in time and he came up short. I don't think he would have swallowed it, but you never know.

Yair said something in Hebrew, must have been a curse of

some sort, and he definitely blanched, but then he regained his composure, picked the diamond up, and put it in the little box.

"That's how diamonds get lost," he said. "They're tiny and you drop them and you're screwed. But you know what we say in the diamond business: when a diamond falls to the ground, it's going to sell."

"Well, it already has," I said. "So where's the cash?"

14.

THE MONEY CAME in thick packets of ten thousand dollars each, wrapped with rubber bands, and Yair dumped it all for me in a paper bag from Whole Foods.

Then he put that bag in one of those large-size reusable Trader Joe's bags, which he gave me as a gift, and I said: "You must eat healthy. Whole Foods. Trader Joe's. I try to eat healthy."

"Only the best," he said and smiled, and we shook hands and our business was done.

By 11:30, George and I were back in the car. I checked my phone and there was 3 percent battery left and more messages about the *LA Times* article, but the only message I paid attention to was from Monica—"How are you feeling? Were you able to rest?"—which I didn't feel capable of responding to.

In her mind, I must have been home, recuperating from having my face and arm sliced open. But in the twenty-four hours since she had dropped me off from the hospital, Lou had died, I had found a blonde man with a bullet in his head, had thrown another blonde man off a balcony, had lied to the police, been beaten by the police and taken to another hospital, visited the house on Belden Drive, which had been wiped clean of dead bodies, ended my four years of analysis with Dr. Lavich, saw Rafi, and sold a stolen diamond for two hundred thousand dollars cash.

So it didn't seem right to respond to her innocent text with something like, "Feeling fine," and so I avoided the whole thing and got the car to the 101, in the direction of Los Feliz and the office of Ken Maurais.

George made himself comfortable on the floor by his seat, next to the Trader Joe's bag of cash, and I didn't have Lou's daughter's address or number, but I'd track her down when the time was right and give her this final gift from her father.

At 11:55, I parked the Caprice on Hillhurst, across the street from Maurais's office, which was in a brown two-story brick cube with large windows and a glass front door.

I gave the place the hairy eyeball, and then George and I got out of the car, and I threw the Trader Joe's bag in the trunk. Then we crossed the street and the butterflies were everywhere, like confetti, and I looked back at the Caprice and decided I didn't feel comfortable leaving the money behind.

So we crossed back over, got the trunk open, and I looped the Trader Joe's bag over my shoulder, like a purse.

Then we crossed again and George urinated on the wheel of a gleaming parked Tesla—I looked anxiously to the right and left for the owner, but no one showed—and then we went inside the brick cube. Maurais's office was on the second floor, up an exposed black metal staircase—the place was going for an industrial look of some kind.

We went up the stairs and on the landing, to the left, was a Farmers Insurance agency and to the right was Maurais's office, behind a glass door.

On the other side of the door was a receptionist, a young woman, blonde and pretty. She was staring down at her phone and then looked up as we came in. "Can I help you?"

"I'm George Mendes. I called earlier. I have a twelve o'clock appointment."

"Oh, right," she said, and her eyes got a strange look as she took in my face and the bandage. "Just have a seat. Ken should be here any minute." She indicated two chairs across from her, against the wall. Behind the young woman was a closed door, which must have led to Maurais's private office.

I sat down, and the girl glanced at George. "Cute dog," she said. "Beautiful eyes. It's like he's got eyeliner."

"I know," I said. "I love him very much."

That made her nod uncomfortably, and then she picked up her phone to study it some more, to kill more seconds and minutes and years of her life, which made me think of my phone and yearn for it.

Which is how it works: you see someone playing with their phone and then you want to play with yours, like an addictive yawn, and so I got mine out and of course the battery was dead.

"Could you charge my phone by any chance?" I asked the young woman, and she said, "Yes," but then Ken Maurais came through the glass door.

He was about five nine, early seventies, and his frosted hair was between dye jobs. It was half gray, half blonde, and he had a big horsey face, losing its fight with gravity. He was nicely dressed in a wool blazer, gray slacks, and a dark purple shirt. George lunged for his crotch and Maurais stepped back, not happy about it.

I then stood up and reached out my hand. "George Mendes,"

I said. "We have a twelve o'clock appointment, but sorry about the dog. He loves good-looking people."

My little joke made Maurais smile, and he displayed a rather large set of white chompers, an expensive implant job. He gave me his hand to shake and it was thin and practically boneless, which is always disturbing.

"Ken Maurais," he said, and as we held hands, George got his nose against Maurais's zipper, but now Maurais didn't mind, and he let go of my hand to caress George and said to me: "What's the dog's name?"

"George," I said, and as soon as it came out of my mouth, I wanted to scream.

"You're both named George?" he asked, sharp on his feet, unlike me, who was doped in two different directions, north with the Adderall and south with the Dilaudid.

But then I rallied, somewhat, and said, "I know it's peculiar, naming him after myself, but more important, I really want to buy a house with a pool and was hoping you could help me."

As a follow-up, I then gave him my best winning smile, and he gave me the once-over, but since realtors are very forgiving of the human race—they have to be to sell houses—he said to the receptionist, "Julie, can you bring us some water?" and then to George and me, he said, "Come into my office."

We followed him in and he had a nice view of Hillhurst, and on the walls were various diplomas and licenses, along with a David Hockney poster of a naked young man, with exposed buttocks, lifting himself out of a Los Angeles pool.

It was a handsome painting—actually a poster reproduction from the Liverpool Museum—but I wondered what Maurais's other clients thought of it. It was certainly bold, and I imagined it gave Maurais great pleasure to sit at his desk and look at the young man and remember old love affairs, which in my own way I was all for: better than staring at a phone.

I put my Trader Joe's bag of cash on the floor and lowered myself into the customer's chair. My face and arm were throbbing, but not too bad, and I could control my jaw swivel if I remembered to. "I like the Hockney," I said.

"I know it's scandalous," he said, easing himself into his chair, "but to me it says: *LA!* And that's what I'm in the business of: selling Los Angeles." I noticed a stack of his FOR SALE signs in the corner: the airbrushed photo of him must have been ten years old.

Julie came in with our waters—two small bottles of Perrier and two drinking glasses—and then left us, closing the door behind her. We poured our drinks and Maurais took a pill bottle out of his blazer pocket and knocked back a tablet with the Perrier.

"Nitro," he said, indicating the pill, with some embarrassment. "Unfortunately my heart is 50 percent butter. Maybe more. Could be all butter. And I've had a busy morning, too much for this ticker."

I wondered what he had been busy with and said: "I like a butter sandwich myself."

"Don't even say it! I could live on bread and butter. Who needs dinner? Just give me the bread. *So* how can I help you, Mr. . . . oh, God, please tell me your name again. I'm so sorry."

"No problem," I said. "It's Mendes with an *s*. The same thing happens to me: I always forget people's names the second they tell me."

"Me, too," he said. "If I don't get a person's name the first time, I can go years without knowing it and it's very embarrassing. Though lately I've mostly given up and just tell everyone I have dementia."

Then he showed me his teeth again and I smiled back, and he said: "So what are you looking for, Mr. Mendes? A house with a pool? Julie did tell me over the phone that you're perhaps looking at the two to three million range."

"Yes, that's right. Or four million."

"Even better," he said, but I could see a little something in his eyes. He wasn't a dummy, this man, and he knew what people with money looked like, what they smelled like, and I wasn't pulling it off. I had come in with a Trader Joe's bag, was wearing old khaki pants and my second-string blue blazer, and there was something very wrong with my face. None of this said rich person. None of this said: I can buy a four-million-dollar house. The one thing in my favor was that George was with me and we had the same name. That might signal rich.

"Where are you living now?" he then asked, gently probing to see if his instinct was correct.

"I'm over in Topanga," I said. "But I need to be closer to Paramount. I direct television and we're going to be filming a series there."

"Excellent. Congratulations. So you're a TV director. Wonderful. That's a nice living... Did you get hurt on set or something? I hope you're all right. That's a very big bandage."

"It looks worse than it is," I said. "Just had a little something frozen off at the dermatologist."

He shook his head sympathetically. "I understand completely," he said. "Every time I go in there, they do that to me. Last time, I told them just freeze my whole face and be done with it. But I love the sun! Always have. I'm a decadent person."

"It's good to enjoy life," I said.

"Yes," he said, and he looked at me shrewdly. He still wasn't buying that I had any money. "And how did you find me, Mr. . . . oh, my God. I knew it a second ago."

"Mendes. But just call me George," I said, and George, thinking he had been summoned, jumped in my lap.

"No, not you George, me George," I said.

"Charming dog," Maurais said.

"Yes. A real lover," I said.

"Right," he said. "And how did you find me . . . *George*?" George looked at Maurais when he said that, wondering what Maurais wanted, and so I put George on the floor to maintain some professionalism, and the realtor continued: "It was a referral? Julie said a client of mine was a friend of yours."

"Well, not exactly," I said. "The thing is, I've been staying in Beachwood Canyon, with a friend, while I house-hunt, and I was walking my dog and I saw your FOR SALE sign on a wonderful house." I pointed to his signs in the corner. "And it doesn't have a pool but it looks like it would have a fantastic view, and I'm very interested in it."

This confused him and made him a little nervous. "Beach-wood Canyon?"

"Yes—2803 Belden Drive."

I saw fear flash across his eyes, like birds in sudden flight. "Oh, there's been a mistake," he said. "That house isn't for sale."

"But your sign was there."

"Well, it's been taken off the market," he said coolly, regaining his composure. "We can look at other properties."

"That's too bad it's off the market. Why?"

"Because the owners don't want to sell. That's why." He was now quite rigid in his chair, and all chumminess was gone.

"So it's empty. What a waste. Do you think if I wrote a letter to the owners, I could convince them otherwise? Tell them it's my dream house?"

"No. They really don't want to sell. There are plenty of other houses for you to consider—"

"But I really do like that house, the view, the neighborhood."

"I'm sorry. It's just really not possible." He looked at his watch. "You know, I have a call at 12:15, so why don't you give me your email, and I'll send you some listings in your price range, and we'll go from there?"

"But I really like that house. So what's the owners' name? It doesn't hurt to write a personal note—"

"Mr. Mendes—" he said, cutting me off, and I said, cutting *him* off, "You remembered!"

I was hoping to get things back on friendlier ground, but he ignored my remark and said, "You can send a note to me and I will pass it on."

Then he looked at me, trying to put it all together: I didn't have money, of that he was sure now, and why was I so hell-bent on *that* house? A house where two dead bodies had been at two o'clock in the morning but were now gone because *somebody* had them taken away. Maurais? He said he'd been busy that morning. Needed a nitro to get over it. And so he had to be wondering if I knew something. Then he looked at his watch again—signaling to me that his phony 12:15 call was imminent—and the whites of his eyes were yellow, the color of butter.

I said, all innocence: "So who do I address my note to?"

"Just address it to whom it may concern," he said sharply,

and stood up. "I really need to get ready for my call." He walked over to his door and opened it. George and I made for the door and then I said: "Don't you want my email for the listings?"

"Just give it to Julie on the way out, thank you," and he herded George and me through the door and promptly closed it. Julie had looked up when she heard her name, and I said: "Mr. Maurais would like my email: it's George Mendes five at AOL dot com. And it's Mendes with an *s*."

I'm still on AOL—I struggle with modernity—and that was the first thing that came to mind. Also, I emphasized the *s* again, like Rafi did, to stay in character, though it was futile, really, at this point, and I added the number 5 to make the email seem authentic, which was also futile, because Maurais knew I was wrong, very wrong, and Julie scribbled this nonsense email address onto a pad, and then George and I left, and Julie went back to studying her phone.

We hit the sidewalk outside of Maurais's building and next door was a small Italian deli attached to a restaurant, Little Dom's. I got a coffee to go to keep the Adderall company, and George lapped at a bowl of water they had for dogs.

Then we got in the car and I chastised myself for not handling things better with Maurais; I hadn't extracted any information from him, except what was unspoken: the mention of the house had spooked him plenty and so he knew *something*. At least I had gotten that much.

My thought then was to plant myself there, follow Maurais when he left, and see if I could get him alone. In a more private setting, I might be able to squeeze something out of him, and I wondered how long I might have to wait before he made a move. Could be hours, and I thought of taking another

Dilaudid or at least half of one; the throbbing in my face was starting to ramp up again.

But then Maurais came hurrying out of the building, looking quickly over his shoulder—maybe for me?—and then he disappeared behind the building into the parking lot.

Julie, when I first called, said he'd be in all afternoon, but now, just a few minutes after meeting me, he was rushing out, heading somewhere with urgency.

Then an old black two-door Mercedes emerged from the parking lot and Maurais was behind the wheel. He made a right and headed up to Los Feliz Boulevard. I got the Caprice in gear, swung a U-turn on Hillhurst, and fell in a few cars behind Maurais. The throbbing in my face was still there, but with adrenaline in my system the pain was noticeably less.

Maurais turned right on Los Feliz and was driving fast, but I didn't lose him, and George, looking brave and sensing something, stood up and put his paws on the dash. He knew the hunt was on.

15.

AFTER LOS FELIZ, the little Mercedes got on the 5, a ten-lane freeway, heading north. Traffic was heavy but moving, and there was no way Maurais would know I was on his tail, though it was important to keep a nice distance and that he not see me. Not too many drivers had big white bandages on their faces or dogs, like sentinels, with their paws on the dashboard.

From the 5, he took the 134, and I thought maybe he was going to Burbank, but then he got onto the 101 North, heading into the Valley, and I started wondering what the hell he was up to. Then we hit some truly nightmarish traffic and George lay down on the front seat; boredom had quickly set in.

It was bumper to bumper, thousands of cars jammed together, going nowhere and somewhere, reaching speeds as high as five miles per hour, ten if we were lucky, and even with the recent rain, the white smog, which we live in all the time, was especially thick, and you would never know that just a few miles to the east the whole valley basin was ringed by beautiful mountains, the San Gabriels.

But they were obscured by the white filth, and it's old news, of course, but we are forced, in this modern life, to always hold two ideas in our mind at once: one, the natural world is beautiful, and two, we are destroying it.

When we passed through Woodland Hills, I had been tailing Maurais for nearly an hour because of the traffic and was growing increasingly worried that wherever he was going had nothing to do with Lou or Dodgers Hat or dead men in a house on Belden and that this was all a big waste of time.

But at least my driving was satisfactory.

I could operate the Caprice without killing anyone.

On the downside, though, my face was being difficult. The adrenaline of the chase had more than worn off, and it was like there were fire ants in my wound, and I said to George, who was half asleep, curled up like a croissant: "Where the hell is this asshole going? My face is killing me!"

In response, George turned and looked at me over his shoulder, and there was a bland sympathy in his eyes; he was in his own bored hell.

Then, finally, as we got closer to the Agoura Hills and Malibu exits, the traffic thinned considerably and the white smog cleared away and the 101 began to roll up and down through beautiful low foothills, empty of man-made structures.

In the fall and early winter, there had been catastrophic fires, wiping out thousands of acres all along here, but this had been followed by weeks of rain and so the landscape was now a mix of blackened trees and swaying grass so green and bright it was almost neon. Birth had followed death.

Then Maurais exited the 101 at Kanan Road, which he took in the direction of the coast. At first, there were a few cars separating my Caprice and his Mercedes, but Kanan quickly becomes a country road, and the cars between us kept going off onto side roads one by one, and it was getting trickier to follow Maurais and not be seen.

So I hung back as best I could and nearly missed him turning right, at a blind curve, onto the Mulholland Highway—I flew right past the intersection—but luckily I caught sight of the Mercedes, out of the corner of my eye, and changed course.

Between us now there was only one car, a white BMW with its top down, and I stayed about a quarter of a mile back.

The Mulholland Highway, despite its name, has only two lanes, and it comes equipped with dark tunnels through mountainsides, hairpin turns, and guardrails you don't want to drive through, unless you're feeling tragic, and all the while, it climbs steadily up its portion of the Santa Monica Mountains for about ten miles.

As we ascended, I would lose sight of Maurais and then spot him for a second when the road evened out momentarily, and behind my sunglasses, I was squinting.

The light, as we got closer to the ocean, was becoming more severe in its clarity, and all around us was beautiful, empty country, the neon grass an inland sea.

But also on the green hills and along the ridges were more and more fire-burned trees, with their blackened, skeletal arms reaching for the sky, frozen in supplication.

Then Maurais and the BMW both turned onto another winding road, Encinal Canyon, which steadily climbed for at least two miles until we crested, and then suddenly the Pacific loomed ahead, planetary in its immensity, and it was breathtaking in the bright sunlight, sparkling like a sea of stolen diamonds.

Then the road began to descend, hugging the mountain on the right, which had outcroppings of boulders and pink rock formations that wouldn't have been out of place in Arizona, and on the left-hand side of the road was a sheer, frightening drop, down into the canyon far below, and then on the left there was a dirt overlook where cars could pull over and take in the view of the ocean.

There were no houses anywhere on Encinal, but about two hundred yards after the overlook, there was a driveway on the right, which Maurais pulled into, stopping in front of a large black gate with a call box.

First the BMW drove past him, and then I followed, glancing to my right, and Maurais's big head was poking out of the Mercedes and he appeared to be talking into the box. The driveway in front of him, which was more like a private road, was steep and went up the side of the mountain at a forty-five-degree angle.

But whatever house the driveway led to wasn't visible. It had to be over the ridge or set back from the ridge, but either way you couldn't see it from Encinal, and as I continued down the mountain, I watched in the rearview mirror as the gate began to swing open; Maurais had been granted access.

A mile farther down the mountain, I was able to make a U-turn and drive back the way I had come. The imposing black gate was closed, and Maurais and his car had disappeared up the driveway. There was a number on the gate: this was 1479 Encinal Canyon Road. If my phone wasn't dead, I could have called Rick Alvarez and asked who lived there.

But that wasn't an option, and for all my bitching about phones, I was going to have to pretend I was in the past, when you couldn't know everything right away and you had to be patient because time was different then. It lasted longer.

I went up to the dirt turnoff and parked the Caprice so that I had a good view of the driveway, not to mention the Pacific, which seemed to stretch halfway to Japan and its leaking nuclear reactors.

It was a little past 1:40—we had been driving for almost ninety minutes—and George and I got out of the car, both of us desperate to urinate.

Blinking in the overbearing sun and using the Caprice to shield us—or me, anyway—from any cars driving by, we passed our water.

I finished before George, and he seemed to make a deliberate point, midstream, of shifting his angle to cover over what I had done, replacing my mark with his mark.

"I can't believe you did that," I said, but he couldn't have cared less, and he pulled on his leash, wanting to sniff about after the long, torturous ride.

So we walked around the dirt overlook, and the wind was cold up there on the edge of the world, high above the sea, but it felt good on my face—it was numbing—and I kept an eye on the black gate two hundred yards away.

And I had the feeling that we might be there awhile, that an old-fashioned stakeout had begun, which George then christened with a well-formed number two.

"Good boy!" I said, and I nudged his offering—without getting any stuck on my shoe—off the side of the cliff, and George, delighted with himself and mentally relieved, joyfully kicked up a lot of sand, with all four paws at once.

16.

AFTER A FEW more minutes of letting George sniff and mark, two hobbies from which he derives great meaning and pleasure, it was getting a little too cold in the wind, and we went back to the Caprice, officially on the next stage of our stakeout: sitting in the car and wondering one thing: What was Maurais going to do next?

Settling in, George put his head in my lap and looked a little forlorn, and I said with concern, "Are you thirsty?" And he said yes from his mind to my mind, and so I checked, but my coffee cup from the deli was empty; I had finished it during the long trafficky quest on the 101.

I thought maybe he could have licked the cup—there was water in coffee, after all—but that wasn't a possibility, and I was angry at myself for not being better prepared.

Dehydration is not good for a dog *or* an out-of-control individual on a variety of pharmaceuticals, and then I remembered that for a few weeks I'd been hearing my old thermos rattle around on the floor in the back and kept not doing anything about it, and I reached over the seat and dug around in a bunch of refuse and came up with it.

I looked down in the well of the thing and there was maybe an inch of stale H_2O, and then I put my nose in the thermos and it didn't smell too bad. So, thinking it was more or less safe, I poured most of the precious liquid into the lid, which serves as a cup, and said to George, "This is it for a while," and he nodded, resolute, like a good soldier, and went at it.

When he was finished, I poured a meager drip into the cup for myself—George's germs didn't concern me—and I drank from it like an old-time ham in a desert movie, and that was it for our water supply. I screwed the thermos closed and dropped it back over the seat.

Then, as the numbing from the wind wore off, the fire ants really started up in my face again, and the pain was a cross between a relentless sting and a relentless throb.

At this point, I hadn't taken a Dilaudid for about five hours, and I got the bottle out of my pocket and stared at it, very tempted to indulge. But if Maurais left all of a sudden and I had to do more driving, I didn't think I could chance another pill just yet, even if I paired it with more Adderall.

So, showing some resolve despite the escalating pain, I hid the bottle from myself in the glove compartment, and I said to George, "Don't let me weaken."

But he didn't bother to answer. He was busy lying seductively in the sun on the front seat, and his eyes, filled with light, were as beautiful as thousand-year-old amber.

I then lasted all of a minute, weakening in record time, and opened the glove compartment and reached for the Dilaudid, but then I remembered that there was something else in there that could help me and not be as debilitating: a tin of pre-rolled joints from the cannabis store.

Inside the tin, unfortunately, there were no whole joints, but there were six roaches I had saved, which I had planned, like a good pothead, to break up and put in a pipe. But this was an emergency.

So I smoked four of them, one after the other, rather furiously, and all they did was amplify the pain tremendously. "Oh, my God," I said to George. "The pot made it much worse!"

He turned away from me, which was his way of saying, "Of course it did," and a long, painful hour passed like this: my face throbbing madly and crying for help, and me wondering impatiently what the hell Maurais was doing up there, and what if his business in Malibu had nothing to do with Belden Drive and Lou being shot and killed? Then I'd really be going nowhere fast.

But it *felt* like his coming here was connected, and I reviewed in my mind the assumptions I had made so far: (1) Maurais knew about the dead bodies and might have even helped get the house in order early that morning, which is why he needed the nitro; (2) my asking about Belden Drive had spooked him, and he'd gone running to the owners of the house—or to someone else connected to what had happened—to tell them I was snooping around; (3) whatever Maurais wanted to talk about had to be done in person, either because he didn't trust the phones or because what he wanted to express was of such seriousness that it had to be said face-to-face.

And so then what was my play? Stick to my original plan and wait for Maurais to leave, follow him, get him alone, and make him talk? Make him tell me who he went to see and what he knows? Or do I go up to the gate and bluff my way in?

Or do I go in after he leaves and see what I discover without him around? Maybe Dodgers Hat and the man with the gray hair who had been stooped over like a vulture would be up there.

The risk with that play was that if it was a client of Maurais's who had nothing to do with Belden Drive or dia-monds or dead blondes, then I would lose Maurais until I could find him again, and in this moment he was still my best lead.

So the smart move was to wait for Maurais and stick to the plan. Best to confront him somewhere without other people around, and if he told me Dodgers Hat was up on that ridge, then I would know what I was walking into and I might decide that the front gate was not the best approach.

Clear on the game plan, I then gave George another little walk, and the cold wind did some good work on my face, and George sniffed the ocean air and seemed very content, and I realized there were no butterflies around, probably because of the wind.

Then we got back in the car and it was a little past three. After a few more minutes of playing stakeout, the throbbing and stinging in my face kicked into an even higher gear, and so I smoked the last two roaches to make it all worse.

George sneezed because of the pot fog, and I cracked the windows and said, "I'm sorry," and he rubbed his eyes with his white paws, which looked like opera gloves.

Then I stared out at the ocean to distract myself from the pain, but with each throb a different image came before my eyes: Carl Lusk, his knife in the air; Lou, black blood oozing out of the puncture in his belly; the tall blonde boy on the floor with a bullet hole in his head, like a third eye; and the other blonde with his neck broken sideways after I threw him to his death.

I was on an unholy streak of dead men, and who was next? Me? And was I a good guy in all this or a bad guy? I had killed two men, and I had more or less killed Lou. That didn't seem to put me on the good-guy side of the ledger.

Meanwhile, the pain in my face was relentless, hateful, and I must have been higher than I realized from smoking all the roaches because then I thought I heard a squeal come out from under my bandage, like the noise a rat makes in a wall, and I said to George, feeling myself getting hysterical, "Something's trying to come out of my face!"

And I had a desperate wish to itch at the thing, scratch it, *something*, and feeling crazy, I eased the bandage off to at least see what was happening, what was coming alive underneath there, and what I saw in the rearview mirror horrified me:

My wound, already disgusting, had become a hideous red-and-yellow tumor the size of a dead baby rat, about four inches long, and it was distended out from my face at least two inches, and down the middle of the tumor was the zipper of black stitches, and along the zipper I could see white pus just starting to crawl out, like maggot eggs, and I said to George, "Holy shit! It's infected!"

Then, as if this would make it all better, I tried to put the bandage back on, but the adhesive had lost its will, and, frustrated, I threw it angrily in the back of the car, and George jumped over the seat and retrieved the thing. Then he hopped back over to the front seat—he was a springy and athletic dog—and he started sucking on the bandage.

"Don't do that!" I said, disgusted, and I yanked the infected bandage out of his mouth and, like an idiot, threw it in the back again, and George, naturally, thought this was a game, and he hopped back over the seat, got his prize, and came back with it and began shaking the bandage back and forth in his mouth like it was a dead animal.

So I yanked it away again but didn't want to throw it out the window and litter, so I put it in the visor above the steering wheel, but that made George jump all over me to get at it, and he nearly clawed my suppurating tumor, and so then I shoved the bandage in the glove compartment and he scratched at that, going nuts, and I said, "Stop it, George! Stop it!"

And I thought I was going to lose my mind, but just then, thankfully, Maurais came rolling down the long driveway, and the black gate swung open. It was almost 3:30, and Maurais made a right onto Encinal, heading for the coast, and I counted to sixty and then followed after him.

George then forgot about the bandage, and he put his paws again on the dashboard and stared ahead intently, like a handsome sea captain at the prow of his ship.

17.

THIRTY MINUTES LATER, we hit soul-crushing traffic on the Pacific Coast Highway, just south of Topanga, and George was asleep, snoring gently, and I had taken to moaning, clutching the steering wheel, and rocking in my seat.

When I wasn't doing that, I was trying not to touch my wound, but every few minutes I couldn't help myself and would probe it gently. There was a morbid fascination with feeling it and I kept glancing at it in the rearview mirror to disgust myself.

Between the elder Lusk and the younger Lusk and two go-rounds of surgery, my face had been turned into a piece of rotten meat. Something found in an alley outside a butcher shop. Behind a garbage can.

To mix things up, stuck in the deadly traffic, I also played, once in a while, with the goose egg on my scalp where Lusk Sr. had kicked me in the head.

But to my credit, I never weakened and reached for the Dilaudid, and at all times, I kept about six to eight cars between myself and the little Mercedes.

In total, we were on the PCH for about thirty miles, with

the ocean to our right, and all along the coast, surfers in black wet suits waited in the water for the last few waves of the day, lined up like crows on a wire.

Things finally picked up a little when Maurais cut through the Palisades and headed east on Sunset Boulevard, but then we hit another dose of excruciating congestion and I thought for sure I was going to lose my mind this time, that this was it, but then I hit some sort of transcendent place with the face pain—like getting used to a teakettle whistle that never shuts up.

Then around 5:30, after two very long hours in the car, Maurais pulled into the driveway of a midsize apartment building on Doheny, just a little off Sunset, in West Hollywood.

As I went past the building, the garage gate had just finished sliding open, and the Mercedes drove in, went to the left, and disappeared beneath the building: it was a basement garage.

The sun was just about down and everything was purple again, which happens in Los Angeles at sunset, either because of pollution or the tilt of the world or the combination of the two, and I kept moving on Doheny. Then I did a U-turn, doubled back, and found a parking spot on a leafy side street kitty-corner to Maurais's building, about midway down the block.

I parked facing his building and looked the place over. It was six stories, made of white bricks, and every apartment on the street side had a sliding glass door onto a balcony, with an elegant green canvas awning for shade.

There were palm trees in front, and a sign in script on the wall of the building said: THE OLIVE. The place looked well maintained and pricey, and I figured this for Maurais's home, maybe because it looked like him. Old and from another time.

I took George out of the car but kept my eye on the entrance to the garage in case the Mercedes suddenly popped out.

We walked up the street in the violet light, in the direction of the Olive, and it was a miracle, but one of the houses we passed had a water bowl out in front for dogs, and George, very thirsty, the poor boy, made a dive for it.

I always love it when people do that for dogs, never more so than at that moment, and I wished I could drink from the bowl myself and nearly considered it. I was dry as hell.

After George had his fill, we went back to the car and watched the building for a few more minutes to give Maurais a little more time to get to his apartment, if this was in fact where he lived. Most likely there was an elevator in the garage that had access to the interior of the building.

My face was still doing its teakettle act, screaming at a high pitch, but I was focused and angrily determined: Maurais was close at hand, and he was going to tell me things.

Then I got out of the car with the bag of money and hid it in the trunk. I left George behind with the windows cracked open, and his eyes, of course, were sad, but I didn't take him with me as I wanted my hands free in case I needed to put them on Maurais.

18.

THE BUILDING ENTRANCE had double glass doors, and at one time there might have been a doorman in the lobby, but instead there was a vestibule with another set of double glass doors, which were locked and kept me from entering all the way in.

On the wall of the vestibule was an old-fashioned brass directory of the residents with their names on little typed cards, and next to each card was a buzzer, a small brass button. There were no cameras.

I saw K. MAURAIS 5F on a card and pushed the corresponding button. Built into the directory was an intercom, with a speaker in the shape of a circle made of many small holes in the metal.

There was no response to my first push of the bell, so I pushed it again, and a few seconds passed, each marked by a nasty pulsation in my face. Then Maurais's distorted voice came through the speaker: "Who is it?"

I pushed a button so that I could talk and said: "FedEx. For Maurais, 5F."

I heard Maurais say, "Oh, God," and he sounded exhausted,

which I didn't blame him for—it had taken us, after all, two hours to drive forty-odd miles from Malibu—and then the lock on the second set of doors clicked open.

I walked across the soft lobby carpet and put my hand in my pocket, on Lou's gun. I pushed the button for the elevator, waited a minute, and then an old man in a wheelchair with an aide behind him rolled out.

The aide, a young Spanish woman, was looking at her phone and didn't notice me and the man in the chair didn't look up. His head was down—he was half-asleep—and I recognized him because of his fantastically large nose. He had been on a long-running sitcom in the '70s and I'd seen him in a bunch of movies, all comedies. That schnoz had made him a lot of money, and LA was like that—ghosts all over the place.

I went in and pushed 5, and then before the elevator could close, a hand shot into the opening, alerting the electric eye, and the door opened back up.

The owner of the hand was a middle-aged woman with a halo of curly red hair. She was wearing a conservative dress and low heels, the attire of a lawyer, I felt, and as she stepped in to join me, I said to her: "Which floor?" I was standing next to the panel.

"Five," she said, and I could see her grimace as she looked at my face. I hadn't forgotten the pain I was in but I *had* forgotten that visible on my cheek was my tumor, looking like a skinned baby rat. I pushed the button, looked straight ahead, and the elevator began to ascend. "Thank you," she said bravely.

We both exited at five and I let her out first, but, unfortunately, her apartment was in the same direction as Maurais's.

I wanted her in and tucked away before I rang his bell in case he made a fuss of some sort, so I walked slowly, and when she got to 5H, she turned and saw me lingering there, not really making much progress down the hall.

I tried to give her a little smile, which I imagined was gruesome, and then she opened up her door and went in.

At 5F, I pushed the bell and stepped to the side, since there was a little glass eye in the door. Then the door swung open wide and I stepped into the breach and when Maurais saw me, he staggered backwards, speechless and scared.

I stepped inside and closed the door, and his eyes bulged. My unexpected presence plus the thing on my face had him literally gasping, like someone in a dream who wants to scream for help but can't get the words out.

"Easy, Mr. Maurais," I said. "I just want to talk to you."

We were in a little entrance alcove, and he leaned over a thin chestnut table, which was a repository for his mail and keys, and he was gripping the table, holding on for dear life, panting, and then he looked up at me, grimacing at the sight of my wound, and said in a nasty whisper: "Get out of here."

I took a step toward him and said: "I need to talk to you about the house on Belden."

He stepped away from the table, backing out of the alcove and into the living room, and he said, "Leave me alone, leave me alone," and then his legs buckled and he went to his knees and then he toppled onto his side, oddly, like half of him wasn't working.

I knelt down next to him fast, and his face was already turning blue. One eye was looking at me and the other was off in the wrong direction.

He was having a massive stroke, and his good eye was staring at me with all it had, and I dug frantically into the pockets of his blazer and found his nitro bottle. I hastily got a pill out and tried to put it in his mouth, but his lips were squeezed tight, and I shouted, "Come on, swallow this!"

But the mouth stayed closed—either he didn't trust me or he couldn't open it—and his one good eye just kept staring at me, like an eye in a keyhole in a prison cell, and I said, panicked: "I gotta call 911."

I stood up and didn't see a landline—this was the Lou situation all over again—and I took the place in with a quick scan: it was frozen in time in the '80s, with a white leather couch, glass tables, mirrors, the color red, the color black, sculptures of Greek torsos.

But no fucking phone!

I knelt back down quick. "Where's your cell phone?!"

He couldn't answer, and he was making little sucking noises through his lips, and I patted his body, but his cell phone wasn't in any of his pockets, and like a fool I tried to get the pill in his mouth again, but he still wouldn't open up, and the eye kept staring at me, with hate and terror, and then all of a sudden his jaw slid out of place, like a typewriter carriage, and half his face went to one side, it was grotesque, and then his jaw slid back into place, and it was his face again, but then his whole body went slack and the lights went off in his good eye—no more terror, no more hate—and I was sure he was dead.

But I started CPR on his chest, and it was like pushing down on a bag of hangers.

Then I got his mouth open—finally—and pinched his nose and put my mouth on his and gave him the kiss of life, but got nothing. After that, I pounded on his chest some more and then I stood up and ran down the hall to 5H. I pressed the buzzer and the redhead came to the door.

"Mr. Maurais in 5F had a stroke. Call 911!"

She looked at me, confused. "What are you doing here?" she said.

"Fucking call 911!" I shouted. "In 5F. The man's dying!"

"I don't understand what you're saying."

Fear had made her stupid, and she couldn't get past the idea that a stranger coming to her door must have something to do with her. I slammed my hand against the wall, scaring her more, and shouted: "Call 911! Maurais in 5F is dying!"

She got it then and ran back into her apartment, and I ran back to Maurais and he hadn't moved and I checked his pulse, just to be sure, and he was gone. No more real estate deals. No more bread and butter. No more looking at that Hockney poster and having secret thoughts.

So I ran out of there like I was on fire. I certainly didn't want to stick around for the cops, and having no patience for the elevator—I didn't want to be stuck in a box—I took the staircase at the end of the hall and ran down all five flights, which was one flight for each dead man I had seen in the past three days: Carl Lusk, Lou, the two blondes, and now Maurais.

I hit the lobby and went calmly across it and didn't encounter any more residents. I walked to the Caprice like I was an innocent man, and it was fully dark out now.

I got in the car and drove us out of there.

In my rearview mirror, I saw flashing police lights. A squad car must have been nearby. I had gotten away just in time. But poor Maurais. My face was the last thing he ever saw. I had scared him to death.

19.

GEORGE AND I went up the steps of my house, and I was counting on him barking in case anyone was inside. In the past, when we came home from a walk and the gas man or somebody else was there, George would know it right away and sound the alarm. But he was silent as he trotted up the stairs and so most likely the coast was clear. Still, I got Lou's gun out just in case.

But the front door hadn't been tampered with, and nobody was inside.

I hid the money in the linen closet—it was too big for the ironing board—and I plugged my phone in by the socket over the kitchen counter. It was almost seven—traffic had been bad from West Hollywood—and I was exhausted and hungry and my face wanted to die.

I gave George some food, finally took a Dilaudid, and spooned some yogurt into my mouth. Then my phone came alive and the thing was loaded.

Text messages. Missed calls. Voice mails. The ones I cared about were from: Monica, Dr. Lavich, Thode and Mullen, Aram (Lou's boss), and Rick Alvarez.

Monica and Dr. Lavich were worried about me, and Monica had tried me multiple times. Aram had called early in the afternoon, wanted to know if I had heard about Lou.

Thode and Mullen needed to talk to me right away, and that was three hours ago.

And Rick Alvarez had done some more digging and had come through, after all, with some very interesting dirt. He had texted me several links—some old newspaper articles about a murder and an old obituary—but I cut to the chase and called him to make sense of it all.

"Where you been?" he said.

"My phone died."

"Did you see the links I sent you? Heard my voice mail?"

"Was too much. Spell it out for me."

What he told me was this: He followed a hunch and looked into the previous owner of 2803 Belden, which the records showed was a woman named Caroline Hagen. Then he did a little research on her and discovered that she was from an old oil family, with plenty of money. He also learned, more importantly, that she had died twelve years ago and that her husband, Eric Madvig, a well-respected doctor at USC, had been arrested for her murder. He overdosed her on fentanyl and claimed it was an accident. His presumed motive: money.

At the time of her death, it had been a front-page story, which I vaguely recalled, but the trial of Madvig, two years later, had been overshadowed, in Rick's opinion, by the second Phil Spector trial.

Spector was convicted of murder, whereas Madvig's high-priced lawyers got his charges reduced to manslaughter. Madvig then did sixteen months at a rich man's jail, an easy sentence, but lost his license and his position at USC, and his reputation was destroyed.

What came next from Rick was the kicker: the law firm that repped Madvig at his murder trial was the same firm in charge of the private trust that owned 2803 Belden.

But that wasn't all he had dug up: Caroline Hagen had owned another property, which was part of the same private trust, and I wasn't surprised to learn that its address was 1479 Encinal Canyon Road, in Malibu.

"So what I figure," Rick said toward the end of his rundown, "is that this Dr. Madvig owns the house on Belden. He must have inherited it from his wife, but because he also killed her, it's in a trust of some kind. Hope this is helpful." He said that last bit with false humility. He knew he had given me good stuff.

"Extremely helpful," I said.

"Wild, the whole murder thing, right?" Now he could let out his enthusiasm.

I was silent, thinking. Then I saw that Monica was trying to call me, but I let it go to voice mail. I was going to have to get back to her, but not yet.

"What's this all about, Hank?" Rick asked, breaking the silence.

"I can't explain it all, but I will. I promise. I'm still putting it together."

"Okay. I understand. And like I told you, we're headed to Costa Rica tomorrow morning. I'll check in with you when we're back."

"Right," I said, "thanks," and Rick started to say something but I hung up. I held on to the phone, still plugged into the wall, charging, and studied the obituary and the news articles

Rick had sent about the trial. Some other very important details came out:

Madvig and Hagen had three boys: Paul, Andy, and John. The boys had their father's name. The blonde I threw off the balcony had a money clip engraved with the initials PM. Paul Madvig.

In one of the articles, there was a picture taken in front of the courthouse downtown, showing the doctor with his three sons, who had stood by his side during the trial. It wasn't the best picture, but I could make out that two of the boys were tall and blonde, and they looked an awful lot like they could have grown up, ten years later, to be the two dead men I had met the night before.

The other son, John, also tall, was dark-haired and a little older, and the doctor himself was short and had a large head. Like a vulture. Like the man who had been driving the Land Rover.

And there was one more very important detail: Madvig was a *transplant surgeon*. World-renowned.

So then I was thinking that the meeting at Belden hadn't been about the diamond at all. The diamond was secondary. It was to be used as payment or proof of funds. For a kidney. For surgery.

That's what the meeting was about.

Lou wasn't raising cash with a fence so he could buy a kidney. He already had a kidney lined up and it came with a doctor.

On Tuesday, in my office, he had said he was looking into the black market, and he mentioned a computer whiz at the motel, a young Pakistani man, who could access the dark web. Then on Thursday, when Lou left me a message, he said that it was all working out, and what this meant to me, as I put it together, was that Madvig was still in business, if you knew how to find him. And had enough money. Or a very big diamond.

But something had gone wrong at the meeting. Very wrong.

So I needed to speak to the computer whiz. The one who must have made the connection. I wanted to find out what he knew and to warn him that Lou was dead. I called the Mirage, and Aram answered in a weak voice: "Mirage Suites."

"Aram, it's Hank."

"Oh, my God, Hank."

"I know. Lou."

"It's even worse than that."

"What do you mean?"

"There was a murder here and a robbery. The police just left. They were asking about you."

"A skinny cop and a fat cop?"

"Yes."

Thode and Mullen. They got around. "Who was killed?" I had to ask the question, but I was pretty sure I knew the answer.

"A young kid. Pakistani," said Aram. "His girlfriend found him this afternoon. Everybody's checking out. Nobody wants to stay here."

"When did this happen?"

"Last night."

"Do you know roughly what time?"

"I watched the security tape with the cops—2:32 is when a man came out of his room. You can't see his face, but he's got the boy's computer under his arm."

"Why can't you see his face?"

"Had a baseball hat pulled down. And I told the cops I didn't know who it was."

"Was it a Dodgers hat?"

"Yeah. Everyone wears Dodgers hats. Even killers...and poor Lou. What happened, Hank? This has been a terrible day. First they came this morning, telling me about Lou, and I could barely breathe, and then this afternoon they find the kid."

"Aram, I gotta go."

"Is there going to be a funeral for Lou?"

"I don't know. I gotta go."

I hung up. Dodgers Hat had been at my house around 2:05, when George and I chased him away. Then he'd gone straight to the motel, about a fifteen-, twenty-minute drive. The kid was a loose thread. Could connect them to Lou.

So Dodgers Hat gets to the motel around 2:25, probably looks things over, but doesn't waste much time. He kills the kid, grabs the computer, and leaves the room at 2:32. Then he drives back, another fifteen, twenty minutes, and texts the blonde—Paul Madvig—at 2:51: *All done. Almost back. Be ready to go.*

"All done" must have referred to the Pakistani boy.

Then I realized George had slipped through the doggie door into his chicken coop off the kitchen and had been barking for a while. I had been so focused I hadn't noticed. Then there was a banging at the front door. I took Lou's gun out of my pocket and moved fast to the kitchen window and peeked out.

It was Monica.

20.

"JESUS CHRIST, HAP, your face! It must have gotten worse overnight."

"It did," I said and let Monica into the house. George came back through his doggie door and started jumping all over her, but she didn't care.

"I've been trying you all day," she said. "Why didn't you get back to me? I've been really worried."

Her face was drawn with concern and anxiety, and it made her scar more livid.

"George!" I said. He wouldn't stop jumping on her. "I'm sorry. I...I had problems with my phone...I should have called."

"I thought maybe you had died or something on the pills. That's why I came over."

"I'm sorry," I said, and feeling the weight of everything, I slumped into my reading chair and George got on my lap.

"Are you all right?" Monica asked.

"I'm okay," I said. "I'm really sorry I didn't call," and even though she was upset, she looked, as she always did, so easy in her body, at home in her body, like all the parts were connected, not fighting each other. She was wearing faded brown corduroy pants and a green corduroy jacket, and she looked beautiful. Her soft brown hair was pulled back tight, showing her cheekbones, and her green eyes were clear, letting you all the way in, hiding nothing.

"You don't look okay," she said. "Did the doctor say your face would get this bad? All swollen and sticking out?"

"It's not supposed to look like this, but I got reinjured."

"What? How'd that happen?"

"I'll try to explain . . . it's complicated . . . but let's take George for a walk. He hasn't had a real walk all day."

We took the usual route—up to Glen Holly and back—and I gave Monica a super-abridged version of what had gone down:

Lou had been shot by an unknown assailant and given me a diamond to sell for his daughter. The same cops who handled the spa case showed up, took me in, and Lusk Sr. worked me over. I got put back together at Presbyterian and then went and retrieved my car. Then I'd spent a good part of the day downtown, selling the diamond, and I apologized for not calling or texting, but I'd been having trouble with my phone. So that's what I told her, which meant I left out everything else, like dead blondes, dead realtors, black-market organ transplants, and some doctor named Madvig who killed his wife twelve years ago.

But even the abridged story upset Monica. She wanted me to sue the cops, and she was pissed at me for not spending the day in bed.

"You're right," I said. "I've not been smart," which was as close to honesty as I could get, and when we came back to the house and went through the gate, George darted at something and put it in his mouth. I tried to get it out, but whatever it was he'd already swallowed it. He was always finding little berries and things, and for the most part I trusted him to know what he should eat or not eat, but as we started up the steps, he began to choke and was twisting his head from side to side, violently.

I picked him up, and he was gasping bad. "George, are you okay?"

"What's wrong with him?" Monica asked, scared.

"I don't know," I said, starting to panic. "Let's get him inside. It's too dark out here. He's choking on something!"

I handed Monica the keys and we ran up the steps, and George was convulsing in my arms, and Monica went in first and I followed her.

In the living room was Dr. Madvig; a tall young man with dark hair and a .22 in his hand; and Dodgers Hat, who was pointing a very large .38 right at Monica.

"Close the door, Mr. Doll," said Madvig, and George went very still in my arms.

21.

"WHAT DID YOU do to him?" I shouted at them, enraged. *My beautiful boy*.

"No more barking now," said Dodgers Hat, and he gave me a hideous smile: his underbite jutted out monstrously, like a birth injury that had never been corrected.

"I'm gonna kill you," I said to him, impotent, and he just smiled at me some more and then pointed his gun at my head. The .38 scared me, but it was better than having it pointed at Monica.

"Put the dog on the couch, Mr. Doll," said Madvig, all calm. "We just want to talk to you. No one will get hurt."

But I didn't move. I was stubborn and confused, George was dead in my arms, and Monica said, scared, "What's going on, Happy?"

"It's going to be okay, Monica," I said, and everyone in the room knew I was lying.

"Put the fucking dog on the couch," said the dark-haired one, who I figured was Madvig's oldest son, John; his only *living* son. Then he swung *his* gun to Monica's temple to emphasize his point. They liked pointing their guns at her.

"Okay, okay... don't do anything stupid," I said. This one looked jumpier than Dodgers Hat, more impulsive, and I walked over to the couch—my back was to all of them—and I lay George down right where Lou had died the night before, and nothing felt real, except one thing: because of me, George was dead.

Then I slowly put my hand on Lou's gun in my pocket, thinking maybe I could do it. Maybe I could get my gun out fast and shoot them all and not hurt Monica.

But I knew it was foolish and I hesitated and then something loomed up behind me, and before I could turn fully, Dodgers Hat chopped the back of my head with the handle of his .38 and sent me to the floor.

Monica screamed and Madvig's son grabbed her violently, put his hand over her mouth to keep her from screaming more, and I tried to get to my feet, to get him off her, but I couldn't push myself up—my body wasn't working; my head was broken—and Madvig kneeled next to me and jabbed a hypodermic into my neck and I went completely prone; my face flat against the floor.

I could see their feet and I heard Monica scream again, she had somehow gotten loose from the son, and I had to get to her, but I just couldn't, I couldn't even lift my head, I was paralyzed, all my strength was gone, and then my eyes stopped working—I was sure they were open but I was blind—and then I slid from this world and the last thing I thought was: *Please don't hurt her.*

PART III

1.

I WOKE UP in a hospital bed.

I wasn't fully conscious at first, but I slowly became aware that my wrists were cuffed to the railings on the side and that my ankles were cuffed to the railing at the end.

I was under a thin blanket and a bedpan was between my legs. I was in a paper hospital gown and an IV drip was attached to my right arm. My left arm, where I had been cut, was freshly bandaged, and out of the corner of my eye, I could see a new bandage on my face.

Then I remembered everything, like an avalanche of reason, and I yanked my wrists to no avail in the handcuffs and screamed out: "Monica!"

My dry voice came out cracked and weak, and the response was silence.

I didn't know where I was, but I wasn't in a hospital, of that I was certain. I craned my neck as much as I could, with my arms secured to the railings, and I could see that I was in a large semidarkened room with a Spanish-tile floor, an old-style stucco ceiling with wooden beams, and a thick wooden door.

Then, twisting my neck, I was able to see that behind me a shade was pulled three-quarters of the way down the room's one window, letting in sunlight along its edge, like yellow fire.

Which meant it was no longer Friday. When they had come to my house, it was dark out.

In front of me, on the other side of the room, there were door-length white-painted shutters that looked like closet doors, and then there was another door, which was open a crack and seemed to lead to a small bathroom. Flush against the wall to my right, in the shadows, was a metal table with medical supplies on it, but there wasn't any other furniture.

Then I tested all the metal cuffs.

I was no Houdini.

I was thirsty and my lips were dry and coated in film. I called out again: "Monica!"

I was hoping she was somewhere nearby and would let me know, but I heard nothing. The only sound was a strong wind hitting the window.

My face was itchy, but there was no pain.

I looked at the IV bag hooked to my arm. They had me on something. Maybe a sedative. There were two other bags on the metal stand, but they were not attached to the port in my arm. What were they? Food? Water? How long had I been like this? And where was I? I was in a house, probably Spanish-style, based on the tile, but where?

Then the wind rattled the window some more and I knew where I was: Malibu. On top of that ledge, where Maurais had gone, the wind would be strong off the ocean. That's where Madvig had brought me. To his house on Encinal Canyon Road. But why? What were they doing? And where was Monica?

I tried to slide my wrists out of the cuffs, but it was no use.

I figured they had kept me alive because they wanted to know if I had told anyone that they had killed Lou Shelton and were on the dark web offering black-market surgeries.

One thing they could be pretty certain of was that I hadn't been honest with the cops, because no cops had gone up to Belden Drive. Madvig and Dodgers Hat must have gone back to the house at some point, saw it was safe, and cleared out the bodies, which meant two things: they knew I had killed the second blonde, Madvig's son Paul, and that I hadn't talked to the police.

But I could have told someone else, and that they would want to know.

Which meant that Rick Alvarez was in danger. He was the only person I had spoken to who could make any link to Madvig. Rick didn't know why I was interested in the doctor, but he knew enough. Enough to get himself killed, and I was cuffed to a bed and they'd be able to get anything out of me they wanted. I didn't kid myself about how brave I might be. I'd give Rick up no matter how hard I might fight, but if I could hold out a little while... he was taking off for Costa Rica today and maybe he'd be all right...

But they had Monica, if she was even still alive, and in frustration, I yanked on my wrists and ankles. I wanted a miracle of strength that would never come, and I raged in the bed, fighting the cuffs like a child throwing a tantrum.

Then I tried furiously to wiggle my right hand out. Wasn't there a way to dislocate the thumb and get free like that? But I knew from being a cop that this was an urban myth. Still, I tried. Maybe it wasn't a myth.

So I yanked my wrist toward myself, trying to put pressure

on the thumb joint, and I fantasized that if I got my hand out, I'd find a pin or a piece of metal and free my other hand and then my ankles...

But all I did was rub a bunch of skin off.

Then I closed my eyes and stopped trying and my self-hate burned like acid.

I had been bitched from the moment I was born. I had brought ruin on everyone and everything I had ever touched. Now Alvarez was going to die, and Monica had to already be dead. They had to have killed her. She was a loose thread, a witness. I was only alive because they needed to know if I had spoken to anyone.

I pulled on all my cuffs again, throwing another tantrum. *Please, God, give me a miracle*, I thought, and just then, Madvig, his son, and Dodgers Hat, who was no longer wearing a Dodgers hat, came into the room. Madvig had on a white doctor's jacket over a shirt and tie; Dodgers Hat was wearing blue nurse's scrubs; and the son was in jeans and a thin leather jacket.

Madvig flipped a switch near the door, turning the ceiling light on, and said, full of cheer: "Good morning, Mr. Doll."

2.

I DIDN'T RETURN his greeting, and the three men crossed the large tiled room and approached my bed, and I got a better look at my captors than I did when they had surprised me at my house.

The son, late twenties, was handsome and fit: his hair was black and sleek, like the wing of a crow. He was at least six two, built like a swimmer, and he looked like he wanted to kill me. He knew—they all knew—that I had thrown his brother Paul off a six-story balcony, and like a wannabe tough guy, he had his .22 tucked into the front of his pants.

Dodgers Hat, in his midforties, was also big, at least six four, 250. He was thick-chested where the son was lean, and he had enormous, meaty hands that hung by his sides, with the fingers slightly curled in.

He had little brown eyes, brown hair, small curdled ears, and a strange nose. It was almost flat to his face, like it had been pushed in early in life when the bone was soft, and his lower teeth, jutting out at least an inch because of his underbite, were gray and packed in tight.

And next to him, Madvig, a small man in his midsixties, looked even smaller.

He was maybe five six, neat and compact, but his head was overly large.

It didn't seem to match his body: it was too heavy and ponderous and it burdened him, making him lean forward ever so slightly, which is what gave him the aspect of a vulture. And his lead-colored hair was very thick, which made his big head seem even bigger.

His nose was also big, Roman and arrogant and dotted with blackheads, and two deep creases ran from his nostrils down to the edge of his thin pale lips. It was an unhappy mouth, and his intelligent eyes were dark under thick, wiry brows.

At my bedside, he put his finely boned hands on the railing near my right handcuff, and he smiled brightly, like a phony, and said: "And how are you feeling?"

He was still playing it all chipper, and he spoke with a slight trace of an English accent, some affectation from his days as a big shot, and he put a purr in his voice, the purr of the *warm doctor,* the one who makes you feel cared for.

I said: "Where's Monica?"

"You know you've had a lot of trauma to the left side of your face," he said, ignoring my question. "The wound was infected, but it's already clearing up. We've put you on antibiotics." He motioned to the IV bag. "And I imagine you were injured the night you killed the football player. We read about it in the paper. You're quite the celebrity."

"Just tell me where Monica is."

He smiled patiently. "She's here," he said. "You have nothing to worry about." Then he hit a switch on the side of my bed and got me into a sitting position. "That's more comfortable for you," he said. "For a conversation."

"She's alive?"

"Of course she's alive."

"Thank God," I said out loud, not meaning to, and Madvig's son smiled perversely. Then trying to cover, I said, "I want to see her right away." And I tried to make it sound like a demand that had to be fulfilled.

Madvig shook his head. "That's not possible, Mr. Doll. We need to talk."

"I'm not going to tell you anything," I said, and I could feel how hollow and pathetic that was, but all I had were clichés. I was chained to a bed.

"But you've already told us everything. Don't worry about that."

I felt the back of my neck go cold, and suddenly there was a shadow in my mind, the sense of something missing. "What are you talking about?"

"Well, you've been very forthcoming, very accommodating," Madvig said. "You've already told us about Mr. Alvarez, who is on vacation and not really a threat, and nothing else was of interest, though the mystery of Ken's death was explained, and thank you for the two hundred thousand dollars, which Ben picked up yesterday."

Dodgers Hat—*Ben*—smiled and said: "Was in the closet, just like you told us."

"What day is it?" I asked, scared of the answer.

"It's Sunday morning," said Madvig.

I had lost thirty-six hours and remembered *nothing* but had told them *everything*. I said again: "I want to see Monica."

"I've already told you that's not possible," said Madvig.

"You have to let me see her."

"No. I want her calm and I want you calm."

"What the fuck are you talking about? Calm? Torture me, whatever the sick fuck you want, but you gotta let her go."

"You're not being realistic, Mr. Doll."

"Well, you're fucked," I said. "The cops are going to come here. They are going to be looking for us."

"We don't want the police here, that's true," said Madvig, "which is why it's time to close up. But first we need to make a little money, which is what I want to explain to you. It's important for you to understand what is going to happen so that you can prepare yourself mentally."

Madvig then took out a pen and began to tap my body with it, in all the corresponding spots, like he was giving an anatomy lecture and I was the cadaver.

"Your kidneys," he said, tapping me on the right side of my body and then the left, before going elsewhere, "will bring in two hundred thousand each, but the second one will wait until we are done with you. Your heart will fetch seven hundred and fifty thousand, your lungs half a million total; we can also repurpose your cornea and middle ear and parts of your small intestine. Some of the organs we'll simply harvest and then sell to fellow practitioners."

"Fuck you," I said, pathetic and helpless, not wanting to believe him—it was too mad. But I *did* believe him.

"There's also your pancreas," he said, "and bone marrow, and, naturally, your liver is quite valuable. I imagine you had no idea how much you are really worth. You're going to save many lives. Help so many people...and your friend—she's even more valuable. Lungs, heart, liver, *ovaries,* but we can't use either of your faces for transplantation. You're both too scarred—"

"Don't fucking touch her!" I screamed helplessly, and I yanked my arms and legs.

"Of course we will keep you both as comfortable as possible for as long as we can. A living donor makes for the most successful transplants, and Wednesday morning will be your first procedure. Someone, who is also O positive, needs your kidney. So it's good timing you're here, but it's an easy surgery and you will recover quickly—"

Then I went truly nuts, fighting the cuffs, thrashing my whole body, and Madvig said: "Stop it, Mr. Doll! I don't want you hurting yourself."

Then to his son, he said: "John, hook up the fentanyl," and to the big man, he said, "Ben, hold him down," and Ben put one of his large hands around my neck, choking me, but I kept fighting: he was going to have to kill me.

And he nearly did.

I felt myself starting to black out: his fingers were like iron, and I didn't want to but I stopped resisting, and Ben let go, and I was gasping, and the son, John, put another line—which must have been the fentanyl—into my arm port, and I said to him, out of breath, but hoping, pitifully, to wound: "Doesn't it bother you that your father killed your mother like this?"

But he just smiled at me, and I looked at the .22 tucked into his pants. "That gun make you feel like a man?"

"Keep talking," he said. "We're going to strip you and sell you for parts."

Then I could feel the fentanyl—it came on all at once; it was like dropping down an elevator shaft, but without fear—and Ben lowered the bed, and the three of them seemed to be standing in smoke, and all the fight had already gone out of me. I only had begging left, and I said to Madvig: "Please let her go."

He smiled beneficently at me but didn't say anything.

Then I whispered, fading out: "Why are you doing this?"

"I lost two sons, Mr. Doll," answered Madvig. "You owe me a great deal. I think this is more than fair."

3.

WHEN I WOKE UP NEXT, the room was pitch black, and I was in a straitjacket and secured to the bed with tight straps across my shins, thighs, chest, and forehead.

I couldn't move at all—they really wanted to make sure I didn't harm myself—and the port had been relocated to my neck, and I was hooked up to something. Probably something to keep me hydrated and fed.

And just to be extra thorough, they had put a ball gag in my mouth to go with my straitjacket.

So I lay there for hours, utterly immobile in the darkness, and thought of prisoners of war being tortured, and I called upon myself to be brave. I tried to be measured in my breathing, to feel each inhalation and each exhalation, and it worked for maybe a few minutes at a time. Mostly there was panic and horror, like a mouse in a glue trap.

And to know that I had brought this on Monica...

At some point in the middle of the night, Ben came in and saw that my eyes were wide open. So he flipped the switch on the fentanyl, and as I began to disappear again, he said: "We won't keep you on this all the time. We want your kidney function to be good. But tonight, I'll let you sleep."

In the morning, he gently woke me and pulled open the shade behind me, flooding the room with light. I was glad that there had been no dreams.

He removed my bedpan, undid the strap across my chest, and unfurled the right side of my straitjacket. Then he grabbed my right wrist and cuffed it to the railing. I didn't have a chance to try anything. Then he undid the left side and got that wrist cuffed.

"I want to wash you," he said. "You going to be good? Not going to yank?"

I was still gagged and my head was still strapped to the bed and so I said yes with my eyes. I wanted to play along. I had to find an advantage.

He removed my paper gown and brought in a bucket of soapy warm water from the bathroom and proceeded to gently bathe me with a sponge.

He even smiled at me with his tormented mouth, happy with his work, and so I began to think that he was simple, somewhere on the spectrum, like Lennie in the Steinbeck novel.

When he was done bathing me, he put on latex gloves and applied an antibiotic cream to the wounds on my arm and face and put on fresh bandages. I was being attended to like a cow before slaughter.

Then he got a paper gown on me, put the straitjacket back on, and restrapped me to the bed. He was very careful, each step, to make sure I was always too restrained to try anything, and he kept the ball gag in my mouth the whole time, the strap of it running just below the wound on my left cheek and around my head.

Then he left the room for a while, and I fantasized that Thode and Mullen would be showing up any minute. It was Monday morning and I figured they would have started looking for me by at least Saturday, at which point one of Monica's friends might have reported her missing. Maybe she had even told someone she was coming to see me.

They'd then make the link between Monica and me, which would make finding me even more urgent—maybe I had done something to her—and I might have been connected, by Saturday or even Friday, to the death of Maurais. The woman in 5H could have easily identified me, and there were surely cameras in the lobby.

So: Monica's disappearance, Lou's death, the Pakistani boy's murder, Maurais—they'd be desperate to track me down, and they'd get hold of my text messages and phone calls from Sprint, which would further link me to Monica and lead them to Rick Alvarez down in Costa Rica, and he would lead them to Madvig.

He'd tell them I had been looking into a Dr. Madvig who had killed his wife and had properties in Beachwood and Malibu.

So they had to come! Even if it was to arrest me because they didn't understand what was going on—let them come!

Then Ben came back to the room, wheeling in a tall, L-shaped tray table with a plate of food on top of it: scrambled eggs, toast, and some fruit. He got my bed into a sitting position and swung the tray over my lap. Then he ungagged me, and because my arms were still bound, he fed me, sitting on the edge of my bed, one forkful at a time. It was my first food since Friday, and I thought for a second of going on a hunger strike but decided it was best to continue to be compliant. To observe him. To find an angle.

"How are the eggs?" he asked. He seemed to enjoy caring for me.

"Very good," I said. "Thank you."

"My secret is a little bit of milk. Put the milk in with the eggs in a bowl and stir it up. Make 'em fluffy."

"You do the cooking, too?"

"Oh, yeah. I love to cook."

When I was finished eating, he had me stand up. I was still in the straitjacket, and he bound my ankles, loosely. "We need you circulating," he said. "Good for your kidneys, your whole body. And we don't want you to get bedsores."

He kept an iron hand on the back of my neck, and with my feet partially bound all I could do was shuffle, and there was no way to escape. I thought momentarily of trying to throw myself from his grip and brain myself on the floor, but if I did that I would be of no use to Monica.

As we turned back to shuffle toward the bed, my legs were a little shaky but not as bad as I thought they'd be, and I was able for the first time to look out the window.

My view was of a driveway, bordered on the left by dark-green grass and on the right by wild grass leading to a cliff edge, and beyond that was the Pacific. Since the bed kept me from getting too close to the window, my line of sight was limited, but I prayed that I'd see Thode and Mullen coming up the driveway at any moment.

After a few minutes of shuffling in the room, with no arrival from the cavalry, Ben got bored and said: "Want to walk around the house?"

"Sure," I said. "It's good to move my legs."

And this wasn't a lie. I had been in that bed since sometime

Friday night and I needed to move. I needed to get strong. That was another angle: regain my strength.

Out of the room, he led me down a long hallway of maroon Spanish tile. We passed two rooms with closed doors—could Monica be in one of them?—and the third door we passed was partially open. I glanced over and could see part of a long metal desk, a boxy white machine of some kind, and a tray of glass tubes filled with blood. I stopped shuffling and said: "What's in there?"

"That's our lab, where we do the blood work."

"Who does it? You?"

"No," he said, like my question was ridiculous. "John handles hematology *and* anesthesiology. The doc does the cutting, and I do the nursing." This was the division of labor.

"And you do the cooking, too. You do a lot," I said, trying to flatter him, get him on my side.

"Yeah. I like to stay busy. Keep moving."

I started shuffling again. "What did the other boys do?"

"They made the runs to Mexico for the transplant drugs and all the other meds. We're like a pharmacy. We offer full service."

He was proud of what they did and had no hesitation about telling me anything. He didn't seem to have a low IQ, but he was guileless and almost innocent. I didn't know how to classify him—simple but not simple?

So maybe there was a way to exploit his nature, to manipulate him, but I couldn't forget, even if he came across as a gentle giant, that he was also violent. He had killed that boy at the motel, and when he came to my house following Lou, he would have killed me. *And* he had poisoned George.

With his hand heavy on my neck, I shuffled some more, and

then the hallway emptied out into the kitchen, which was no longer a kitchen.

It had been transformed into a makeshift nursing station with everything you might find in a hospital, and beyond the kitchen—and even more disturbing—was a large high-ceilinged dining room that had been tented off and remade as a surgical triage unit. This nightmare was much too real, and I knew the answer, but I asked Ben: "What goes on in there?"

"That's where the doctor uses his gift," he said with great reverence, and to the left of the tented room were two French doors, which seemed to lead to an outdoor area.

"His gift?" I said.

"Oh, yeah, he likes money, like anybody, but really all this is because he loves the work. They never should have taken his license away."

He clearly worshipped Madvig, an utter sociopath, and careful to keep the disgust out of my voice, I said: "How did you meet him?"

"In a halfway house," he said. "I'd just finished ten years at Lancaster for armed robbery, and he'd had his little vacation at the rich man's country club, but they put us in the same house in Ventura, and when we got out he took me in and sent me to nursing school, and the rest is history."

All this pleased him very much, this story of their friendship, and then he shuffled me around some more and on the other side of the kitchen was a large living room minimally furnished with a few chairs, a couch, a dining-room table, and two wheelchairs lined up against the wall.

There was also a fireplace and a wide staircase to a second floor, with a sophisticated chairlift, and I had a feeling Monica was up there. I was tempted to call out, but now was not the time; Ben and I were getting along; this *had* to be to my advantage. But I did say, "Is that where you're keeping Monica?" and with my arms locked in the straitjacket, I indicated, with a nod of my head, the upstairs.

"Yeah," he said. "She's got a nice room. Nice view."

"Is she okay?" I asked, my voice unintentionally quavering.

"She's doing good. She's a good girl. But let's not talk about it."

"Are you treating her all right?"

"Don't worry about it," he said, showing some annoyance, and it was involuntary, but I fought back tears at that moment. Monica was just up those stairs, beyond my reach. She had to be terrified. How could I have done this to her? Then I thought: *I've got to stay focused; don't give over to despair; take everything in; there's got to be something I can use…*

And as we crossed the living room, I got a good look out the big picture window directly in front of me: there was an expanse of lawn and a long, rectangular pool, and on the other side of the pool was the back of another Spanish-style house, even bigger, which must have been their living quarters, and so this must be the guest house. A very large guest house.

I could also see more of the driveway than I was able to from my room—it ran between the two houses, with flagstones along its edge, and on the driveway, near this house, was the Land Rover. Seeing it sparked a meager bit of hope: I just had to get out of this straitjacket, take care of Ben, free Monica, get the keys to that car, and…

He shuffled me back to the room, gagged me, and strapped me to the bed.

Then he got the bedpan between my legs and threw the thin blanket over me. "Try to rest," he said, tucking the blanket under my chin. "You've been through a lot."

4.

HE LEFT ME alone in the room, and I lay there, staring at the ceiling, and I figured there were two ways to go: the slow game or try something now.

It was Monday morning and Madvig said the surgery would be Wednesday morning. That gave me roughly forty-eight hours if I were to play the slow game, which was to work on Ben and wait for an opening that may or may not come.

The one time his good mood seemed to crack was when I brought up Monica and so maybe that was his weak spot—he felt guilty about her, pitied her.

So how should I play him? Keep humanizing her, talking about her, until I could persuade him to let her go?

And if I saw him every meal before the surgery, which seemed to be the most likely schedule, that gave me five more times with him over the next two days.

Or maybe less, because they would probably have me start fasting at some point before the surgery. Which meant I might only see him four more times.

And he was a talker, which was to my advantage, but was I even capable of manipulating him?

He was clearly loyal to Madvig, and to free Monica or free both of us was to cut his own neck. He wasn't *that* simple and I wasn't *that* skilled at manipulation, which meant, I decided, I had to try something *now*. Which was for the best: locked down on that bed I didn't have the patience—or the sanity—to wait.

And it was too risky to wait.

I only had forty-eight hours, maybe less, and once they cut my kidney out, I'd be too weak to do anything and at some point they'd start cutting into Monica.

So now was the time, and for the rest of the morning, I kept thinking about how Ben had unfurled the straitjacket before bathing me. He had started with my right side and my right hand, my stronger hand. Maybe that was my opening. And I started visualizing how it could happen.

Next time he bathed me, he'd probably follow the same order—unfurl the right side of the jacket and take hold of my right wrist. My head would be secured to the bed, and I would have almost no leverage, but as he grabbed my wrist, I'd break free of his grip and grab *his* wrist. This would surprise him: he'd be caught off guard, and I'd yank him down to my chest with everything I had. The strength of my whole life.

Then I'd get my arm around his neck and choke him out. He was strong, but so was I. And I was desperate. I had thrown Madvig's son off a balcony. There were resources in me that were untapped, and once he was unconscious, I'd be able to free myself with my right hand from the straitjacket and undo the straps that secured me to the bed.

All this required him to bathe me again, and to that end, I was able to squirm just enough to get the bedpan off to the side a little. Then I did feel my stomach activating after he'd given me that breakfast, and I tried to force a bowel movement and I wasn't successful at first, but then one happened. It felt like a lot of it got on the bed and between my legs, and it was disgusting lying there, but it was the least of my problems.

At least three hours passed as I lay there in my filth, but I practiced in my mind over and over again what I would do. What I *had* to do. I couldn't count on Thode and Mullen, though I was still praying they'd find us.

But until they showed up—*if* they showed up—I had to try something.

Finally, Ben came back to the room to feed me lunch and when he got near me, he knew what happened. "Smells like somebody went," he said happily. "That's good. Got you back on real food."

Then he put my lunch tray down and pulled back my blanket to remove the bedpan. He saw the mess I had made and said, "Damn," and I moved my chin as much as I could and tried to talk behind the ball gag, indicating I wanted him to remove it, which he did.

"Can you bathe me again?" I asked. "I'm sorry that happened; the bedpan shifted or something."

"It's all right," he said, and then he took the blanket all the way off me and threw it to the floor. Then he took the bedpan to the bathroom, ran some water in there, and came back with the bucket and the sponge. The mess was all over my paper gown, which stuck out the bottom of the straitjacket, and so he was definitely going to have to take the jacket off. This was my chance.

He released my chest strap and then unfurled the right side of the straitjacket, just like before, and grabbed my wrist, which is when I pulled it away hard, with everything I had, and it *did* surprise him, *did* catch him off guard, and my hand was free and then I grabbed his wrist—it was going just as I had visualized it—and I tried to pull him down, and that's where it all fell apart.

He simply grabbed my wrist with his left hand—he was standing and he was powerful and had all the leverage—and he yanked my hand away, got it in the cuff, and locked it. "Everybody starts off a fighter," he said, not really annoyed. "But then they learn."

I was out of breath. But then I said: "Who's everybody?"

He unfurled the left side, grabbed my wrist violently, and got it cuffed. I asked him again: "Who's everybody?"

"The donors. People like you. In the beginning, they fight and then they get tame, become good patients."

I felt sick and I said: "Is that why you have this straitjacket?"

"Yeah. At first we thought we'd pay people—you know, illegals; whores if they had good blood work." He threw the straitjacket on the floor and ripped the gown off me. "But then we realized pretty quick that paying them was too dangerous. They'd talk if we let 'em go. So we had to trick 'em."

He took off all my straps, spread-eagled my legs, and cuffed my ankles to the railing at the end of the bed. I was naked and cuffed to the bed like the letter *x*. "How'd you trick them?"

"We'd show 'em the cash, make them feel secure." He yanked the sheet out from under me and threw that to the floor. "But then when we got 'em here, we'd hold on to them. Harvest them, like you. And then when they realized what was going on, they'd all fight." He squeezed the sponge in the bucket and started cleaning me between the legs. "So we got the straitjacket and the restraints so you don't hurt yourselves.

But everybody learns. Better not to fight and I'll take good care of you."

"How many donors have you had here?" I asked, and what I meant was: How many other people have been in this jacket and never gotten away?

"Only twenty-three," he said as he sponged me. "But they saved a lot of people. The doc says that if it was mandatory for every motorcyclist to be an organ donor there'd be enough to go around, but there isn't enough. Not even for rich people. Which is where we come in. With us they don't have to wait on line, but everything's fucked now. Things are too hot. But I can't complain. We've made plenty."

He straightened up from his work and rubbed his thumb and forefinger together and gave me a gruesome smile.

"You've killed twenty-three people?" I asked.

He nodded and resumed cleaning me.

"You're sick," I said, craning my head to look at him.

"Don't be mean. You're hurting my feelings," he said. His little eyes were merry on top of his flattened nose, and he pushed his jaw out even farther, pretending to pout.

I looked at him and a terrible hopelessness pushed down on me, and I said, a weak man: "Just don't do this to Monica. *Please.*"

He didn't say anything to that, but he put the gag back in my mouth—suddenly he was tired of talking—and he continued to bathe me, as gently and as patiently as he had before.

5.

WHEN HE FED ME LUNCH a little while later, we didn't speak. I was fully restrained again and I forced the food down—tomato soup and a grilled cheese sandwich—to keep alive my illusion that I had to maintain my strength to stay ready...but ready for what? How could I possibly get out of this?

After lunch, he gagged me, lowered the shade, hooked me to the IV for hydration, and left the room. I lay there and began to play in my mind, on an endless loop, my failed escape attempt, and then I came up with a new plan.

I'd pull my hand away—I had done it once; I could do it again.

Then I'd shove my elbow down to the bed, bringing my hand down alongside my chest. I'd extend my fingers out hard, turning my hand into a knife, like I did when I got Carl Lusk in his eye, and then Ben would have to bend over a little to grab my wrist. That would bring him in range, and I'd dart out my hand, my fingers firm, and I'd jab him hard in the throat, collapsing his windpipe and putting him out of commission. I visualized the move over and over. *It could work!*

This went on for what must have been hours, this fantasy, but then I began to itch everywhere, uncontrollably; it was most likely psychological, but maybe I was also having withdrawal from the fentanyl, which I hadn't had since the night before.

So I started writhing to relieve the itching—tiny movements were all I could manage, wiggling like a worm in the jacket and beneath the straps—and then I started feeling like I was choking on the ball gag; I couldn't get myself to breathe through my nose, and my tongue was pushing hard against the ball, trying instinctively to get it out of the way, which made things worse and seemed to make my tongue swell, and so it was my own tongue I was choking on.

And the more I choked, the more panicked I became, and I rocked and rocked trying to get some relief, to get away, to break free, to stop the itching, to breathe, anything, until at some point, worn down, I passed out.

When I woke up, it was very dark in the room and it seemed that Ben must have decided not to wake me and had skipped my dinner.

And so I just lay there, but I couldn't control my mind and the claustrophobia returned, and I began to choke, terrified again of swallowing my own tongue, and so once more I began to shake and thrash, and then I realized that the straitjacket had been loosened.

I couldn't believe it, but I was able to pull my right arm out! Then I removed the straps across my head and chest, was able to sit up and get the ball gag out. Ben must have freed me! My talking about Monica had gotten through to him after all!

I then pulled out the feed from my neck port, but I didn't know how to remove the port itself without causing a lot of bleeding, and so I left it in my neck.

Then I undid the other straps, got out of the bed, and ran to the door. I opened it a crack and listened. Nothing. Then I went out into the hall—it was dark—and I trotted quickly, in my bare feet, down to the kitchen. From there, I went cautiously into the living room and one lamp was on, giving some minimal light, but no one was around.

I then went up the stairs as quietly as I could.

To the right of the second-floor landing was an unusually long hallway with a window at the end letting in moonlight.

I could make out several doors along the hallway and behind one of them had to be Monica.

I opened the first door and the room was empty.

I opened the second door and Ben and John were sitting on a bed, smiling at me.

"I just wanted to fuck with you," said Ben.

I stared at them and then I ran down the hall and hurled myself down the stairs.

"Don't you fucking run!" screamed Ben after me.

But I had a head start. I got out the front door and the moonlight was strong, and I ran up the driveway in my bare feet and hospital gown.

I looked back, and Ben and John, furious, had just emerged from the front door.

There was no way I could outrun them, and so I went to the cliff's edge to the right of the driveway and hurled myself down the hillside, my feet ripping, but I had to get away. I had to! Then I'd come back with the police for Monica!

But the hillside was steep and I began to tumble, losing my balance, and then it became a paved embankment, which didn't seem possible, and I fell and rolled down it, painfully and out of control, until I landed at the concrete bottom, alongside the edge of the Los Angeles River. The water, black and silver, reflecting the night sky and the moon, was high after all the rains and was moving quickly in its concrete riverbed.

Then I looked up the hill and Ben and John were scrambling down it, and I had nowhere to go, so I jumped into the river and it was freezing cold, and it began to take me along, and I was fighting not to drown, but then I got control of my body and was able to swim or at least stay afloat while the current hurled me downriver.

But then, sensing something, I looked behind me, and the water was suddenly rising up like an ocean wave, a tsunami wave, and then it peaked, high above me, an immense dark curtain of water, and I couldn't get away, I couldn't move, and then it came slamming down on top of me, pushing me to the bottom, and I looked up and the water was roiling above me and would never let me back to the surface, and I couldn't breathe, I was going to die, and it was then that I had the double horror of realizing I was dreaming, that there would be no saving Monica, no getting away, and that what I would be waking up to would actually be worse than drowning, and it was then that I came out of the dream, choking beneath the ball gag but still alive.

6.

ABOUT AN HOUR LATER, Ben showed up to give me dinner. I had been wrong about that in my dream.

He put the bed in the sitting position and kept me in the straitjacket.

And I welcomed his presence. I didn't want to be alone in that room anymore, in the darkness, strapped to the bed. I was already getting Stockholmed and was scared by the idea of him leaving me again.

But I wasn't completely slavish, not yet.

I had been fooled by him in my nightmare, but I knew—or wanted desperately to believe—that he had some sympathy and feeling for Monica, and so I had to try to exploit this. It was my only gambit.

He swung the tray table in front of me, sat on the edge of the bed, and began to patiently feed me a salmon patty, mashed potatoes, and a salad. I was very passive and quiet, which pleased him, and after a few bites, I said, like it was no big deal, like none of this was a big deal: "How's Monica? She doing okay?"

"Yeah, she's fine. But I told you already, we're not talking about her."

"Okay. Okay." I ate some more and then I said: "I won't talk to you about her, but you know, the cops are going to find us. They're going to find my friend in Costa Rica, and talking to him will lead them here."

"Not going to happen," he said good-naturedly.

"It is and you should let Monica go before they get here."

"Shut up," he said.

I shut up for a few more bites and then I said: "Listen to me. Grab the two hundred thousand I got for the diamond and take off. But let Monica go first. Come on—you don't want her to be hurt. I know it."

He put the fork down and said, genuinely angry for the first time: "Stop talking to me about the girl. Eat your food. Or I'm going to fucking make you go to sleep."

I finished the meal in silence—I wasn't a very good manipulator—and as he rolled the tray away, I said: "Why do you do this for Madvig? Kill people? Hurt Monica?"

He turned to me, pissed. "Why do you think? I do it for the money, asshole. And let me give you some advice: stop dreaming about any cops coming to save you two. We've got friends down south who we do a lot of business with and so you and the girl crossed the border into Mexico on Saturday—in your car—and you've been using your credit cards, having a good time, and then when we give the go-ahead in a few days, two burned corpses with your IDs are going to turn up, and then there's going to be a mix-up in the morgue and the bodies will be cremated. So nobody's looking for you, because they think they know where you are, and then you're going to be dead. Except you're not. You're going to be here making money for us."

Then he flipped the switch on the fentanyl and put me down for the night.

7.

IN THE MORNING, Ben bathed me again and I tried to pull my hand away, my second big escape attempt, so I could jab my fingers into his voice box, and it went nowhere. With my head strapped to the bed, I had no power, and Ben swatted my hand away like it was nothing. He was back to his genial self, and he said: "You'll stop fighting after tomorrow," and I wanted to say something like, "I'll never stop fighting," but I had spouted enough clichés, and the truth was I wondered if I had *already* stopped fighting.

After breakfast he took me for a walk, and I said: "Can I ask you a question?"

"About the girl?"

"No."

He shuffled me down the hallway. "Then you can ask."

"Why'd you kill my friend—the old man?"

"I didn't kill him; Andy did."

We came into the kitchen–nursing station. "I figured as much, but why did Andy kill him?"

"That old man pulled a gun on us."

"But why? Why'd he do that?"

"The doctor looked at his records from the VA and gave him an exam and said he was too much of a risk to die during surgery. We can't have the patients die here. Too many questions."

"And with donors there's no questions?"

"That's right," he said, and he laughed.

"But why'd my friend pull the gun?"

"Because he still had to pay the twenty-five thousand consulting fee, except he wouldn't. He yanked out that nasty Glock, said he wasn't paying, and tried to back out gangster-style."

So it was how I imagined: Lou pulling the gun, backing into the elevator.

We went across the living room and stared out the window at the pool. "Me and the doctor would have let him go," Ben continued. "It was only $25K, but Andy was carrying—he and his brothers, they like their guns—and I couldn't believe it, but he shot the old man and the old man fired back. Straight-on head shot. No more Andy. Then your friend, the old man, got away and everything has gone to shit since."

Just then a large black BMW pulled up in the driveway, and John, whom I hadn't seen since Sunday, popped out of the driver's side. Then he got a wheelchair out of the trunk, unfolded it, and opened the rear passenger door. An old man emerged, whom I recognized, and John helped him into the chair.

I had a terrible feeling, and Ben said: "That's where your kidney's going, buddy. Better get you back to your room. We don't want to spook him."

He started shuffling me back across the living room, and I managed to wriggle away from him, some last-ditch crazy hope, but bound at the feet and wearing the straitjacket, all I did was fall hard to the floor.

Ben lifted me up and looked at me, concerned. But I hadn't injured myself.

"You shouldn't have done that," he said.

Then he started shuffling me back to my room, his hand tight on my neck, and he said, not without sympathy: "I'm sorry, buddy. What can I tell you? The rich like to live forever."

"I guess they can afford to," I said, playing the tough guy, cracking jokes, and Ben laughed, and I knew who the rich man was. He was the actor with the big nose from Maurais's building. All those sitcom episodes were going to pay for my kidney, and it must have been more than real estate that Maurais had brokered in.

We got to my room and Ben strapped me to the bed and when he went to gag me, I kept moving my head, making it hard for him.

"Quit fighting me. I know you—you'll scream and upset the old man."

"I won't. That's not it. Just let Monica go, please. You have me. She won't—"

But he didn't let me finish. He held my head down violently, gagged me, and left the room.

He then checked on me a few times during the day, playing with my IVs and keeping me hydrated, but then that stopped: I couldn't have any more water, nothing, and all I could think about was Madvig reaching his hand inside my body and snipping out my kidney.

8.

THEN THAT NIGHT, trapped in the jacket, gagged, and alone in the dark, I lost it in a good way and had some visitors, one after the next:

My mother, whom I only knew from photos, but she was so glad to finally meet me.

My father, who had changed completely—all his anger was gone.

Lou, who got me into all this trouble in the first place, and, of course, he was smoking.

George, my sweet boy, who kissed me over and over.

And then a real surprise visitor: the first girl I ever loved, Sarah.

She was my girlfriend when we were seventeen and she'd had the most beautiful smile. She was one of those illuminated people. Light came out of her and everyone felt better when she was around.

But when I went into the Navy, she went to the East Coast and we lost each other. In my twenties, I heard she got married and I wondered if it could have been me, and then in my forties, I heard she had died of brain cancer and left behind a little girl.

I couldn't believe this had happened to her—not *Sarah!*—and it was so painful to realize that I had missed out on her whole beautiful life. Why did I let that happen? Why couldn't we at least have been friends?

But then there she was in that dark room, holding my hand, smiling at me, like she still loved me, like she had never stopped loving me.

And I was so happy to be with everyone who came to see me. It all felt very real. They were right there with me, sitting on the edge of my bed, and I said to each of them many times, I love you, I love you, I love you.

9.

I SOMEHOW SLEPT for a few hours, and in the morning, I woke up, probably around dawn. I was still strapped to the bed and soon I was going to be operated on against my will and I had to try *something.*

I had to go down fighting, and I began to imagine Madvig talking to me before the surgery. Doctors always tell you what they're going to do before they do it, and they'd have to unstrap me if they were going to cut me, and I could lunge for him then and get my mouth on his neck and rip out his jugular; I had seen something like that in a movie. *What did I have to lose?* Or maybe I might even get away and be able to save Monica. Kill him and the other two could fall.

So I started practicing in my mind and passed a few hours like that, and then Ben, wearing a surgical mask, came into the room and wheeled me out of there on the bed, still strapped down and gagged.

He rolled me all the way to the surgery tent, where Madvig and his son, in masks and scrubs, were waiting for us. There were bright surgical lamps blinding me and Madvig said: "Good morning, Mr. Doll. This'll be over before you know it, so not to worry. Kidneys are very tiny, not more than five inches, so they slip right out."

Then he said to his son, "Let's get him started," and John hooked me up to the IV, inserting the feed into my neck port, and he said, "I'm going to count down from ten," and he began, and they weren't giving me a chance to do *anything*!

They were going to unstrap me and ungag me *after* I was out, and John was saying, "Nine, eight, seven," and Ben took my hand at the bottom of my straitjacket and gave it a warm squeeze and said, "You're going to be okay," and I could see that beneath his mask he was smiling at me with his twisted mouth.

When I woke up three hours later, I was short one kidney.

10.

I WAS BACK in my room and Ben had changed my restraints.

I was no longer in the straitjacket—probably because of the incision on the side of my abdomen—and I wasn't cuffed to the railings with metal bracelets.

There were still straps across my body and my head, but I was now lying on a pad with Velcro cuffs, which secured my ankles and wrists, and because I was pinned to the pad by my own body weight and the straps across me, I was utterly immobile. I had seen such rigs in psychiatric hospitals when I was a Navy cop and then later in the LAPD. They were effective with violent psychotics.

But I wasn't gagged and I tried to scream for the hell of it, except my throat was a dry rasp. I lay there for a while, still feeling heavy and thick from the sedation.

Then I tried to scan my body, to see if I could sense that my kidney was gone, and I thought I felt an absence, like a drawer had been removed from a dresser. Then I dozed off for a little while, but woke back up when Ben came into the room. He said: "You like the new setup? More comfortable than a straitjacket. Was delivered this morning."

I just looked at him, and he lifted up the bandage on my abdomen and said: "Looking good. You and the old man did great. How's the catheter feel?"

"Catheter?" I couldn't lift my head, strapped as it was to the bed, and so I wasn't able to see between my legs, and I had no sensation down there.

"I'll take it out later," he said. "We got to make sure you can piss on your own."

I closed my eyes and he went to the bathroom. He came back with a cold compress and dabbed it against my brow.

I looked at him and said: "How's Monica?"

"Jesus. Don't start that again."

"I want to start it again. What does Madvig have planned for her?"

He looked at me and smiled. "Okay. You want to drive yourself crazy, I'm gonna tell you. Next week we're gonna need half her liver. The good news is it will grow back if we need more."

I closed my eyes again. Then I said, looking at him: "It's not too late. You could let her go. You got me. Just keep cutting me up."

"She's a different blood type, asshole. B positive. We need her." Then he put the ball gag back in my mouth to shut me up and played with my IV. "Since I'm a nice guy," he said, "I got you morphine. Make you feel good."

A few hours later, he woke me up and got the catheter out, which felt like a razor was being drawn across the inside of my penis, even with the morphine in my system. Then he had me urinate in the toilet and I was weak as hell, and he said, "You got good waterworks."

Then he strapped me back into the bed and turned my brain off with the morphine, knocking me out, and I was glad to go away.

The next time I woke up it was night and the door was open and a shaft of light was coming in from the hallway, and Sarah was standing over me in the half darkness and her hands were on my shoulders, shaking me, and I said, "I'm so glad you came back."

And she said: "Can you sit up?" Her voice was a panicked whisper and I realized that there was blood all over her face.

"What happened to you?" I said, concerned.

And she said, whispering fiercely: "Happy, wake up! Wake up!"

And then she turned toward the door, afraid, thinking she heard something, and some light caught her profile and I saw a scar, and I realized it wasn't Sarah. It was Monica!

"Monica," I said, and I wasn't dreaming. Not at all. Monica was in a paper gown just like mine except her gown was covered in blood.

She turned back to me and said: "Can you get out of bed?"

I nodded yes, and she put her arm around my shoulders and helped me get to a sitting position. She had already undone my straps and I wasn't connected to the IV.

"What's happened?" I said, slowly coming more awake.

"We have to get out of here," she said, her eyes wild. "I killed the son. I killed him. We have to go!"

She helped me stand and I was a little wobbly but I could move.

We made our way down the hall. "Faster, Happy," she said, and I tried, and we were both in our bare feet, and we got to the living room and headed for the front door—light from the pool outside, with its underwater bulbs, made the room glow—and she said, "Come on, Happy, let's go, let's go," and I was trying to move as fast as I could, but I was still half drugged, and then there was an explosion of sound, a gunshot, and the living-room window blew out, there were shards all around us, and Monica dove behind the couch, and I turned, frozen. I was standing next to the fireplace, and John was at the top of the stairs, naked.

He was holding his gun in his left hand and his right hand was on his neck and there was blood all over his torso, leaking from a gash just below his jawline.

"Don't fucking move," he said, and a cold ocean wind blew through the demolished window, waking me more, startling me, and I was next to the little stand that held the tools for the fireplace: a poker, a shovel, a small ash broom.

John came down to the bottom of the stairs, holding the gun on me, and said: "That fucking bitch."

And I grabbed the poker and flung it at him.

I got lucky and it winged just right and struck him across the chest, scaring the hell out of him, and he dropped the gun, and we both went for it.

I moved quickly, adrenaline surging, but he got there first and as he leaned over for it, one hand still on his neck, I tackled him, and we both went down, and he didn't have the gun, and then we were fighting for it, it was right in front of us, and his body was slick with blood, and the incision in my side ripped open, and then Monica was standing over us with the poker and she brought it down on his head three times, real fast, and he stopped moving and would never move again. She said: "He tried to rape me."

Then she helped me up and I got the gun, his .22, and

then we both heard something and turned and through the shattered window, we could see Ben.

He was wearing sweatpants and sneakers—the spotlight had been turned on—and he was running down the driveway from the front house, a double-barrel sawed-off shotgun in his hand, and Madvig was behind him, in a robe, trying to walk quickly, and he had a rifle. Even with the wind, they must have heard, across the lawn, the sound of the shot and the broken glass, and then Ben fired and the shotgun blast slammed into the house.

"We have to go out the back," I screamed, and I fired once through the broken window, but the .22 was no good at that distance, and we ran for the French doors to the left of the surgical tent.

On the other side of the doors was a back patio with chairs and a table, and it was tucked at the bottom of a sloping hill. There was a spotlight on the patio, casting an arc about twenty yards up the slope, and we went running across the patio and up the slope in the freezing cold, and it was covered with wild grass and rocks—it rose at about a thirty-degree angle—and we just had to get past the rim of the light, where it would be very hard to see us.

But I started to struggle: blood was pouring out of the incision in my side, and my legs weren't really working, I couldn't get up that hill, and Monica was way ahead of me, moving fast, and then she slipped into the darkness—there seemed to be an outcropping of some boulders up ahead—and then a shotgun blast fired right next to me, kicking up dirt, and I turned and fired—Ben was down on the patio—and I missed, and then somehow I got into the darkness, and Monica cried, "Over here," and she was crouched behind the rocks, and Ben fired again, but I was with her, covered, and then another shot fired, followed by silence—he must have been reloading—and I peered around the rocks and Ben was starting to make his way up the hill, in the middle of the arc of light, and Madvig was on the patio, directly behind him, huffing, holding his rifle, and I fired at Ben and it punched Madvig down.

I had shot Madvig in the face and he went straight back, falling to the ground. Ben shrieked and ran back to Madvig, and I fired at him twice and missed both times, and he put his shotgun down and picked Madvig up and ran through the French doors, carrying Madvig in his arms like a child, and I shot at him two more times, missing him again, and then the clip was empty.

"Let's go!" said Monica, and she went running down the hill, and I followed after her, holding the empty gun, but I still couldn't move fast. She ran around the side of the house and I followed.

We came around to the front and Monica was racing up the lawn alongside the driveway, and I was a good twenty yards behind, and then I heard a noise: it was Ben running out the front door after me.

But I couldn't move at all now.

My legs were dead.

I had been drugged for hours and was bleeding profusely, and I threw the empty gun at him and he rammed into me, knocking me to the ground.

He straddled my chest and punched me in the face, and my poor wound erupted yet again, and then he began to choke me, those huge hands around my neck, and his eyes were enraged, I must have killed Madvig, and the port in the side of my neck was squirting blood, and Ben was getting very far away, he was killing me, and then Monica hurled herself at him, and he let go of my neck and swatted her away, and she went facedown into the grass, and I was able to rise up and his neck was exposed, and just like I had practiced in my mind, and just like I had with Carl Lusk, I drove my hand, like the blade of a knife, into his Adam's apple, and I could feel it explode in his neck, it was a perfect strike, and he toppled off me and fell to his side, gurgling, his hands grasping at his throat, and his legs were kicking spastically in panic, and I stood up and Monica stood up, and she got a large flagstone from the side of the driveway, and she was going to bring it down on his head and put him out of his misery, and for a second his eye caught mine, we knew each other, and then his eye went dead, and his legs stopped kicking, and Monica dropped the rock; it was no longer needed.

EPILOGUE

IN THE END, I made out all right.

The lucky streak that began that night with throwing the poker just perfectly at Madvig's son kept on coming, like a once-in-a-lifetime run in cards.

Looking for a landline in the main house to call the cops, we found a phone in Madvig's office, but we also found his safes—there were two of them—and we changed our plan.

Both safes were about five feet high and deep, and on a whim, I tried both handles—I had learned a long time ago, when I was a cop, that people are often lazy and don't lock their safes. They just close them without going through the necessary steps, and sure enough the second safe had been left open.

We cleared out nearly $500,000 in cash, took the Land Rover, and stashed the money at Monica's house, using her key under the mat to get in.

After that she took me to Good Samaritan Hospital downtown and it was then that we called the police, and, overall, I did pretty well with the law. Thode and Mullen were happy to see me, if you could call it that, and I got charged with a number of things that didn't stick, though I did lose my PI license.

But on the upside, the *LA Times* and the local news affiliates credited me and Monica, not the LAPD, with exposing what Madvig had been up to, and the story went national.

At first the internet went the most wild when it was revealed that it was the old actor with the big nose who had bought my kidney—he had been found alive in the back house, up in Malibu—but then the bigger story twenty-four hours later was the police digging up twenty-five bodies on Madvig's property: the twenty-three donors, who had been murdered, plus the two sons who had gotten killed on Belden Drive. Which was one part of my story I left out: throwing Paul Madvig off the balcony.

Of the money we grabbed, I gave $200K to Lou's daughter for the diamond, and the rest went to Monica, which she accepted and has begun to slowly launder with Rafi at the pawnshop.

After we got that process in place, I took her out for an intimate dinner at a little French restaurant downtown, Mignon, and I said, as we drank our first glass of wine: "I have to say it again: I'm so sorry for all I put you through."

She shook her head and said: "Stop saying you're sorry, Hap. You've said it enough. I mean it."

I nodded and sipped my wine, and then I blurted out, because I'm a fool: "Then there's something else I want to tell you. I'm crazy about you. Could I... could I court you?"

That came out all stilted and weird when I had been aiming for chivalrous and respectful, but she rolled with it. She looked down, thought about it a second, and then, looking up, she told me that everything that had happened was what her girlfriends would call "a big red flag." Probably the biggest of all time. What with nearly getting her harvested for organs being the tip of the iceberg.

"So for now all I can handle is being friends," she said. "I'm just so glad we're both alive."

I nodded my understanding and, of course, she was right.

And what she was offering—friendship—was much more than I deserved and plenty to be grateful for, and I said: "I completely understand. And just so you know, I'm going to keep on working on myself...and if it's all right with you, I'll leave the porch light on. Just in case."

"Leave it on," she said, and there was something in the tone of her voice and the way she looked at me that gave me a flicker of hope.

Then a few days later something else special happened. An elegant handwritten letter arrived from the old actor, thanking me for saving his life. It couldn't have been more lovely and gracious, and we subsequently spoke on the phone and hit it off, and when he's no longer under house arrest we plan to meet. I always did like him in that sitcom when I was a kid.

And the biggest, craziest, unexpected Ace in my lucky streak was that George wasn't dead. He had been badly poisoned and his whole body had shut down, but later he had managed to crawl through his doggie door out to the chicken coop and was discovered by a neighbor, who heard him crying.

She then rushed him to an animal hospital and, thankfully, after just a few months of vitamin K therapy to clean his blood, he's made a complete recovery, is as full of joie de vivre as ever, and still seems to love me despite everything I put *him* through. In fact, we've never been more in love with each other. It's like a second honeymoon.

I've also started up my analysis again with Dr. Lavich, which we're both happy about, and I've even gone back to work, calling myself a Security Specialist. You don't need a license for such a thing, but it can be a way to help people, just like a PI, and because of my notoriety, business has never been better. I do have a nasty scar on my face, but in my line of work that's not such a bad thing.

So, like I said, in the end, I made out all right.

All it cost me was a kidney.

DON'T MISS HAPPY'S RETURN, NEXT YEAR, IN

THE WHEEL OF DOLL.

FOLLOWING IS AN EXCERPT FROM THE NOVEL'S
OPENING PAGES.

One of my flaws is that I'm a great one for asking questions, but I'm mediocre-to-poor at answers. Which isn't the best trait for a detective.

Though it may be why, of late, I've become an armchair Buddhist.

In Buddhism, you're meant to question everything, including the idea of questioning everything.

And really there are no *answers,* anyway.

But that's in nirvana. Which is where you get to go when you become enlightened. I hear it's very peaceful there.

But in this messy realm—the realm of women and men and all their myriad problems—there are *some* answers to *some* questions.

You can figure *some* things out.

Which is why you need detectives. Even mediocre-to-poor ones like me.

Because finding a killer can be like finding an answer.

But I'm getting ahead of myself.

The afternoon when all this began, it seemed like just another nice, cold Los Angeles day—and by cold I mean sixty-five degrees—early in 2020. January third, 2020, to be exact, a Friday.

It was around 4:40 and I had just left my house and gotten into my car, a 1985 royal-blue Chevy Caprice Classic, once the preferred vehicle for police forces around the country. In the twentieth century. Which was a long time ago now and not just in years.

I started the Caprice and let it warm up a second, since it's an old car like an old man, and it always needs a moment to gather itself and get its pants on. But despite its age and three hundred thousand miles, it's not ready to die. Very few of us are.

To pass the time, I lit a joint.

Then I took a sip of coffee from my thermos. I'm one of those people—maybe the only one—that lives on coffee and pot and small fish: pickled herring, sardines, and kippers.

As I took a second sip, I put the radio on, which was already tuned to 88.9—a strange college station, my favorite—and then I took another hit of my joint and another sip of my coffee, and feeling that wonderful alchemy of the cannabis and the caffeine—you're ready to go somewhere but don't care too much if you make it—I backed out of the garage and rolled down my dead-end street, Glen Alder.

I was on my way to my office to meet a potential new client—we had a 5:30 appointment—and I needed the business.

From Glen Alder, I turned right onto Beachwood Canyon Drive, and a black Challenger with tinted windows, parked on the corner, swung in behind me, reckless-like and urgent, and I felt a small tingle of alarm.

Since marijuana doesn't make me paranoid, except when I

eat it, I had to assume that the tingle was coming—like a pre-conscious telegram—from that special part of the brain that knows things before it knows things. But that part of the brain doesn't use words. It uses feelings. Like *foreboding*. And *fear*.

Then again, I told myself, a muscle car like a Challenger isn't great for a tail job—it's too conspicuous and sticks out too much. *So maybe it is the pot,* I thought. *Nobody would follow me in that car.*

Or maybe whoever was in the Challenger didn't care if I spotted them. Maybe they didn't care about being discreet, which could make them cops. Undercover but showing themselves. The undercover units like muscle cars, and so it was worrisome if it was detectives. The LAPD wasn't fond of me. Hadn't been for a while.

I tried to see who was driving the car, but the sun—which was already starting to set—was glinting off the Challenger's windshield, just about blinding me, but I could distinguish that there were two shapes in the front seat.

Which would make sense if they were police. They always travel in pairs.

When I turned left on Franklin, the Challenger turned left, which wasn't so unusual, one goes right or left there, and I told myself to forget about it. Told myself I was being jumpy.

Franklin has four narrow lanes and I went to the far-right lane, nice and slow, which is often how I drive—senior citizen–like and methodical, because I'm usually smoking a joint, like I was just then, and so I try to be extra careful, giving myself plenty of room for error and delayed marijuana reaction time.

But I also drive slowly because I try, as a fledgling student of Buddhism, to be mindful.

I try to do that thing where when you're driving, you're driving; like when you're washing the dishes, you're washing the dishes.

The result is that between the mindfulness and the marijuana, I'm an annoyingly slow driver, and yet the Challenger didn't get into the left lane to pass me, as numerous other cars did.

And now that we were heading east, with the sun at a different angle, I could see who was maybe following me: a white male was on the passenger side and a brown-skinned man was driving. And they looked large and wide. Too big for the front seat of the Challenger. So maybe they *were* detectives. Cops often come in large.

They were close on my tail, and I opened my window—it was getting pretty hazy in the car from my joint—and I sent them an obscure smoke signal, written in Cheech and Chong, which didn't merit a response.

So there we were, my Caprice and their Challenger, meandering like a tandem—*if* we were a tandem—down Franklin, and my office was five minutes away on Vermont, but wanting to test something, I hung a quick right onto Garfield Place without putting on my signal.

Following so close, the Challenger seemed to take the turn a little late, but still managed to make the right onto Garfield and have it look *somewhat* intentional.

Fifty yards later, I pulled over to the side of the road.

They drove on past, feigning disinterest, I imagined.

But because of their tinted windows, I couldn't get a look at the white man on the passenger side, which was frustrating, and maybe it was all a coincidence.

So I just sat there, smoking, and watched the muscle car

make its way down Garfield, a street of squat apartment buildings, and the light in the sky was violet-hued and beautiful. The sun must have just dipped into the Pacific, cooling itself and turning Los Angeles, as it did each day, into a purple city.

Then the Challenger crossed Hollywood Boulevard, disappearing from my line of sight, and so I did a quick U-turn and headed back up to Franklin.

Five minutes later, I turned right on Vermont, went down two blocks, and then parked my car in the quiet, narrow alleyway behind the Dresden bar.

I put my joint in the ashtray, grabbed my thermos, and as I slammed my door, it didn't really surprise me to see the Challenger coming down the alley, glowering in its dark paint job.

I could have run or gotten back into my car, but there was the feeling that I would only be delaying the inevitable, and so I waited for them in the beautiful light. It was what they call in the movie business *magic hour.*

The Challenger parked right behind my Caprice, blocking it, and the two men boiled out, moving fast for their size. They were both about six four, 250, like brother slabs of beef in a meat market.

The white beef looked like a farmboy from the Midwest, and the brown beef looked Hawaiian. Midwest had blonde hair buzzed down like a peach, and Hawaii had black hair pulled back tight in a ponytail.

They both were wearing jeans and sneakers and hoodies, and they had that look. A look that said they wanted to hurt someone. That someone being me.

I did a quick scan of the alley for witnesses, but we were

all alone. On the plus side, these two didn't seem to be cops. Their eyes were too eager: violent but maybe not cruel.

So I put my thermos on the roof of my car, like it was a casual thing to do, and I fingered the steel baton I was carrying in my sport jacket pocket, because I needed *something* to even the odds. There were 500 pounds of them and only 190 pounds of me, most of it alchemized silvery fish from a can.

"You boys seem to know where I live and where I work," I said, as they came to the front of the Challenger, about six feet away. "How can I help you?"

I pegged them to be in their early thirties, and I called them 'boys' because I was fifty-one and missing a kidney, which made me more like sixty-one. When you lose an organ, you lose a decade of your life, someone told me. Which is probably not true but it's a good line when you're looking for sympathy.

"Yeah, you can help us," said Midwest. "You can help us remember Carl Lusk."

That's when I knew for certain the baton needed to make an appearance, and I brought it out and snapped it to its full sixteen-inch length. It's one of those extendable steel batons you can buy on the internet if you're a wannabe fascist or in the security business like me.

Midwest saw my weapon but it didn't scare him—probably because he had never been hit by one—and he took two big steps forward, with his fist cocked, and as he threw his haymaker, I took a step to my right and slashed down on his wrist, breaking something, and he went straight to the ground, mewling.

Then Hawaii charged me, going for a tackle, and I squatted and swiped at his knees with the baton and heard a nice crunch, which made him come up short and fall, but he still was able to knock me to the asphalt, and I landed hard on my ass, with half of him on top of me.

I then hit him brutally across the back of his broad shoulders, which he definitely felt, and I was able to push him off, like pushing off a piano, and Midwest was still on his knees, wailing; his hand was hanging from his wrist at a weird angle.

I stood up, a little slowly, panting from the adrenaline and the fear and hitting the ground hard, and Hawaii also stood up, quicker than I expected, and he punched me in the face, a nice shot to the right cheekbone, and I staggered back and faltered, which made him hopeful.

He then rushed me with a looping punch and I jumped up—I don't know where the instinct came from—and I hit him on the top of his head with the baton, like chopping a piece of wood, and he went down face-first into the pavement.

He wasn't knocked out, but he didn't get up. He curled into a ball, grabbed the top of his head, and vomited. Then I looked around. My fight with these two had lasted less than a minute, and the alleyway was still empty: no one had seen anything.

I didn't want to go near the vomit, and so I limped over to Midwest and he looked up at me, like a child.

His pain had made him innocent again, but not too innocent, and I raised the baton up into the air, like I was going to strike him, but I was just bluffing, playing the tough guy, and I said, "Give me your phone."

He obediently reached into his hoodie pocket with his good hand and gave me the phone. I bypassed his code, hitting the word EMERGENCY in the lower-left corner, and put it on speaker.

"I called 911," I said. "Keep me out of it and I won't press charges. And I won't hit you again."

I handed him the phone—we could both hear it ringing through the speaker—and he just looked at me; he was in some kind of shock, holding his arm out away from his body, like it scared him, which I could understand. His hand was dangling off his wrist like a dead bird, and I said, "I'm very sorry about Carl Lusk."

And I meant it.

Then a woman's neutral voice came out of the phone: "This is 911, what is your emergency?" Midwest then put the phone in front of his mouth, looked at me, and mumbled, "I've been in an accident."

Satisfied, I grabbed my thermos off the Caprice and went quickly through the back door of the Dresden. There was time enough for a swift drink before my meeting, and I wanted some ice for my face.

ABOUT THE AUTHOR

Jonathan Ames is the author of *I Pass Like Night; The Extra Man; What's Not to Love?; My Less Than Secret Life; Wake Up, Sir!; I Love You More Than You Know; The Alcoholic; The Double Life Is Twice as Good*; and, most recently, *You Were Never Really Here*. He's the creator of the HBO series *Bored to Death* and the Starz series *Blunt Talk* and has had two amateur boxing matches, fighting as "The Herring Wonder."